The Lost Expedition – Asterra 9

A Torlan Tarsen Adventure

The Lost Expedition – Asterra 9

Russell V McFall

Ordained Path Books

Published by **Ordained Path Books**
For permissions or inquiries, contact:
ordainedpathbooks@gmail.com

Cover illustration and interior artwork generated by AI under direction of the author.

First Edition

ISBN (Paperback): 978-1-972724-06-4
ISBN (Hardcover):

Printed in the United States of America.

Version 1.00 -- April 2026

Dedication

For my family,
who first heard these stories long before they were written,
and who taught me that the greatest journeys begin at home.

Contents

Chapter 1 — Return to Quiet Ground

The flight back from Havenfall was quieter than the one that had taken them there.

That was not because there was nothing to say. In some ways, there was more to say now than before. Too much, perhaps. Havenfall had not been a simple mission. It had not been the kind of work a person could finish, shake off, and neatly put behind them. Too many lives had been hanging in the balance. Too many decisions had mattered. Too many moments had come down to a narrow line between disaster and survival.

And yet, as the transport descended through the morning sky toward Bill's estate, the silence inside the cabin felt natural.

Comfortable, even.

Alex sat by the side window and watched the land rise slowly to meet them. The morning light lay clean across the fields below, touching the long stretches of grass and the darker lines of trees beyond. From above, the property looked less like an estate in the grand, polished sense of the word and more like a place built for use. It had shape and order to it, but not decoration for its own sake. Everything below seemed placed for a reason.

A landing field spread out in a flat section near the main structures. Beyond it stood several low buildings of steel, stone, and composite paneling, each one clean-lined and practical. A larger central house rested farther back on a rise, broad without being showy, its long windows catching the light. Gravel roads curved between the buildings in gentle lines. Farther out, fenced areas, storage sheds, open ground, and a long equipment structure hinted at work still in progress.

Nothing about it looked careless.

Nothing about it looked like a rich man's attempt to impress people.

It looked like Bill.

Alex found herself smiling faintly at the thought.

Across from her, Bill sat with one arm resting against the side of the cabin, watching the same view with the calm expression he brought to almost everything. He did not look tired, exactly, but the last mission had left its mark. There was a quietness in him this morning that was different from simple rest. He carried silence the way some men carried tension. It did not weigh him down. It simply settled around him until he was ready to speak.

The pilot's voice came through the cabin speaker. "Approach vector confirmed. We'll be on the ground in two minutes."

Bill gave a single nod, though the pilot could not see him.

Alex glanced at him. "You know, most people would probably take a few days off after something like Havenfall."

Bill looked over. "This is a few days off."

She let out a small laugh. "That explains a lot, actually."

He almost smiled.

Almost.

The transport lowered further. The engines softened as the pilot brought the craft over the landing area. Dust stirred beneath them in a slow circle. The landing struts touched down with a gentle jolt, barely more than a shift in weight, and the engines began to wind back.

For a moment neither of them moved.

It was not hesitation. It was the kind of pause that comes after long strain—when the body recognizes safety before the mind fully catches up.

Then Bill rose.

Alex stood with him, and together they moved toward the rear hatch.

As the door opened, cool morning air rolled into the cabin carrying the scent of grass, damp soil, and sun-warmed metal. After the enclosed atmosphere of transport decks, orbital platforms, and command rooms, the smell of open ground felt almost unreal.

Bill stepped down first.

Alex followed him onto the landing field.

For a moment she simply stood there.

She had seen the estate before in reports and passing references. She had heard it described more than once, usually with some mixture of curiosity and disbelief. William Arden's private property. William Arden's private landing field. William Arden's secure operations complex.

The phrases had created one impression.

The reality created another.

There was space here. Real space. Room to breathe, to think, to move. The kind of space that did not come often in stations, offices, government towers, or urban districts where every square meter had already been assigned a purpose and usually three arguments besides.

A light wind moved across the field, stirring the grass along the edges of the packed landing surface. Somewhere farther off, a machine hummed for a few seconds and then went quiet. Birds moved in the trees beyond the main road. The whole place felt settled without feeling empty.

Alex turned slowly, taking it all in.

Bill, meanwhile, had already picked up the single duffel he had brought with him and was looking toward the house as if he had been gone no longer than an afternoon.

She looked at him again. "You really do live like this."

He shifted the bag to one hand. "I told you I did."

"You did," she admitted. "I just wasn't sure what that meant."

"And now?"

She looked toward the long equipment building, then the fenced storage area, then the house again. "Now I think it means that if someone asked you to build an operations center, a workshop, a landing site, and a home all in the same place, you would say yes and then quietly do it before anyone else had finished planning the committee."

This time he did smile, faintly but unmistakably.

"I don't like committees," he said.

"I had gathered that."

They started walking away from the transport as ground personnel moved forward to receive the craft. There were not many people, only a small team, but Alex noticed immediately that they were efficient without being hurried. No wasted movement. No confusion. The pilot climbed down and spoke briefly with one of the crew near the edge of the field. Another was already checking the landing gear and fuel connections.

Bill did not interfere. He acknowledged them with a nod and kept moving.

That, Alex noticed, told its own story.

Whoever worked here did not need him hovering over their shoulders to prove he was in charge.

The gravel path leading from the landing field curved gently toward the main rise. Small stones shifted underfoot with a clean, satisfying crunch. To the left stood a low storage structure with wide doors open to reveal organized racks of tools, cases, field kits, and replacement components. To the right stretched a broader expanse of open land that looked partly maintained and partly left as it was. Beyond it, at the far line of the property, a stand of tall trees framed the horizon.

"Do you ever stop building things out here?" Alex asked.

Bill glanced toward the equipment structure. "Sometimes."

"That sounded unconvincing."

"It depends what you mean by stop."

She smiled. "I thought so."

They walked a few steps in companionable silence.

It was different now than it had been when they first met. Back then, their conversations had carried an understandable caution. Alex had been measuring him, not only professionally but personally, trying to decide what kind of man stood behind the reputation, the quiet intelligence, and the unusual independence. Bill, for his part, had not exactly made things easy. He had never been rude, never needlessly closed, but he had the habit of speaking only when there was something worth saying. That could make him seem distant until a person learned how much he noticed.

Havenfall had changed that.

Shared pressure tends to strip away unnecessary uncertainty. By the time people have weathered real danger together, they usually know more about each other than months of polite conversation could ever reveal.

Alex glanced over at him as they walked.

He looked as he always did—steady, broad-shouldered, composed. At six foot five, he gave off the impression of strength even in stillness. But it was never merely size with him. There was density to him. Control. The kind of physical presence that made every movement seem economical because nothing in him was wasted. He did not move like a man trying to prove he was capable. He moved like a man who already knew.

What made him unusual, though, had never really been his size.

It was his mind.

Alex had seen intelligence before. She had worked around gifted analysts, brilliant engineers, disciplined strategists, and quick-talking political minds who could fill a room with impressive language. Bill was something else. He saw structure where others saw fragments. He could take in a flood of details, strip them down to what mattered, and reach a clear conclusion with startling speed. Not recklessly. Not arrogantly. Just accurately.

And, perhaps most unnerving of all, he rarely seemed aware of how extraordinary that was.

"What?" he asked without looking at her.

She blinked. "What?"

"You're studying me."

"I was thinking."

"That usually means you're studying something."

Alex shook her head with a quiet laugh. "And this is what makes you difficult."

He glanced over. "Only difficult?"

"Would you prefer I broaden the description?"

"No."

"That seems wise."

They continued up the path toward the house. The structure looked even better from this angle. It was wide and solid, built to withstand weather and time rather than chase fashion. Stone columns framed a covered entry. Long windows overlooked the open land below. A side wing extended toward what appeared to be office and communications rooms, if the antenna line and reinforced paneling were any indication.

Alex slowed a little.

Bill noticed. "Still organizing?"

She gave him a sidelong look. "Is it that obvious?"

"Yes."

"That's unfortunate."

"It's useful."

She let out a soft breath and looked around again. "I'm trying to decide whether this place is one good week away from becoming a functioning operations hub or whether it already is one and you simply haven't admitted it out loud."

"It depends on the scale."

"That is not a denial."

"No."

They reached the broad stone steps leading to the front entrance, but Bill did not turn immediately toward the door. Instead, he continued along the side path that ran parallel to the house and opened onto a wide overlook beyond the rise.

Alex followed.

From there the estate spread out below them in full. The landing field sat clean against the green expanse. The lower buildings formed a sensible pattern around access roads and storage lanes. Farther off, sunlight touched the edges of fencing, the roofs of work sheds, the tops of utility towers, and the distant line of trees. It was not extravagant. It was not decorative.

It was alive with quiet purpose.

Bill set his duffel down by the railing and rested one hand on the weathered wood.

Alex stood beside him.

For a while neither spoke.

The silence felt earned.

At last Alex said, “Havenfall feels a long way away standing here.”

Bill looked out over the land. “It does.”

“But not entirely.”

“No.”

That one word held enough weight to tell her he had been thinking the same thing.

She folded her arms lightly. “Do you ever do that?”

“Do what?”

“Finish something difficult, come back somewhere calm, and then realize your mind hasn’t arrived yet?”

Bill nodded once. “Usually takes a little while.”

She smiled faintly. “Good. I’d rather not be the only one.”

“You aren’t.”

That settled something in her more than she expected.

A breeze passed over the rise, cooler here than below. Alex brushed a strand of hair back from her face and watched the transport crew finishing their work in the distance.

“Havenfall changed things,” she said.

Bill did not answer immediately. He tended to give important thoughts room before speaking.

Finally he said, “Yes.”

“That was not exactly an elaborate analysis.”

“You didn’t ask for one.”

“No. I suppose I didn’t.”

He turned slightly, leaning back against the railing now. “You’re thinking about what comes next.”

She gave him a look of mock offense. "It's irritating when you do that."

"Do what?"

"Sound as though you are casually observing the obvious when in fact you are three steps ahead."

"I'm one step ahead."

"That is not believable."

His expression remained calm, but she could see the trace of amusement there again.

Alex looked back over the estate. "Yes. I'm thinking about what comes next. Havenfall put your name in front of more people. Serious people. Some of them helpful. Some of them likely less so. The kind who hear about competence and decide they should immediately attach themselves to it."

Bill said nothing.

She continued, more thoughtfully now. "You know they're going to start reaching out."

"Yes."

"Requests. Consultations. Missions. Partnerships. Probably invitations you don't want."

"Yes."

"Some from people who mean well."

He nodded.

"And some from people who hear 'William Arden' and assume that means they can borrow you, your resources, your judgment, and your time whenever it suits them."

"Yes."

She lowered her arms and looked at him. "You make that sound surprisingly bearable."

"It isn't."

That made her laugh.

"There you are," she said. "I was waiting for the honest part."

"That was the honest part."

"The repeated 'yes' was not?"

"That was also honest. Just less complete."

Alex shook her head. "You realize most people use more words than this in normal conversation."

"Most people waste more words than this in normal conversation."

She opened her mouth as if preparing a response, then stopped and laughed again despite herself. "You know, that would be much more annoying if you were wrong more often."

"Probably."

They stood in silence for a moment, both looking outward again.

Then Alex said, "If this is becoming something more—and I think it is—we need to think ahead."

Bill did not resist the statement, which told her he had already been considering the same conclusion.

"A pilot," she said. "Eventually a dedicated one. Not always borrowed transport and whoever happens to be available."

He kept looking out over the land. "Maybe."

"A logistics manager."

He glanced at her. "That sounds dangerous."

"It sounds necessary."

"It sounds like paperwork."

"It is paperwork. That's how civilized people keep important things from falling apart."

"Civilized people also create a lot of paperwork that doesn't keep anything from falling apart."

"That," she admitted, "is unfortunately true."

She stepped away from the railing and turned to face him more fully.

"Support staff, at least a small trusted group. Some structure. Not bloated, not bureaucratic. I know you don't want that, and honestly, I don't want it either. But if you keep operating at the scale you're beginning to operate, you will either build support intentionally… or it will form around you badly."

Bill considered that.

It was one of the things Alex respected about him most. He did not reject a point merely because he disliked its implications. If something was true, he would sit with it, even if he would have preferred it not be.

After a few seconds he said, "I don't want people standing around with titles pretending to be useful."

"I know."

"I don't want an organization that exists to maintain itself."

"I know."

"I don't want meetings about having meetings."

Alex raised a finger. "On that point we are united in spirit."

That earned the faintest crack in his reserve again.

"But," he said.

"But," Alex agreed, pleased he had said it first.

He looked back across the property. "A pilot makes sense."

She tried not to sound too triumphant. "It does."

"Eventually."

"Of course. I can pretend patience for at least several minutes."

He ignored that. "Support roles depend on trust."

"Agreed."

"And size matters."

She blinked. "That sounded more aggressive than I think you intended."

He looked at her.

She folded her arms, waiting.

After a beat, he said, very evenly, "You are making this conversation more difficult than it needs to be."

Now she laughed outright. "I'm helping."

"You are not."

"I am helping with morale."

"That is not the same thing."

"It often is."

He let out a breath that might almost have been a laugh if someone less careful than Alex had been listening. Then he nodded once toward the buildings below.

"We start small," he said.

There it was.

Not surrender. Not enthusiasm. Just a decision.

Alex felt a quiet satisfaction settle into place.

"Small," she said. "Trusted. Practical."

He nodded.

"No decorative positions," she added.

"No."

"No vice presidents of strategic atmosphere."

He looked at her.

"No directors of conceptual synergy?"

"No."

She sighed. "You take all the fun out of institution building."

"There was no fun in it to begin with."

They fell quiet again, and this time the silence carried a different tone. Not reflective now, but forward-looking. Havenfall had been one thing. What came next might become something larger. Alex could feel it—not in dramatic terms, not as some grand declaration, but in the quieter way important realities usually arrive. Not with trumpets. With structure.

A place.

A purpose.

A handful of good decisions made early enough to matter.

She looked at the buildings, the field, the roads, the house, and then at Bill standing beside the railing with the morning light across one shoulder.

This is becoming something real, she thought.

The idea did not unsettle her.

It steadied her.

After a while she said, "If this is going to become a functioning operation, it probably needs a name."

Bill looked at her as though she had suggested they paint the moon.

"A name."

"Yes."

He turned fully now, facing her with the patience of a man preparing to endure something unfortunate. "Why?"

"Because people name things."

"That doesn't mean they should."

"It helps."

"How?"

"It makes communication easier. It gives shape to an idea. It lets people refer to something without saying 'Bill's place' or 'that private field and work complex near the house' every time they bring it up."

"Those seem clear enough."

"Bill."

He folded his arms.

Alex could already tell she was winning, not because he was convinced but because he had chosen to remain and argue instead of walking inside.

"That look," she said, "is not the look of a man who has a better solution."

"My better solution is not naming it."

"That is not a solution. That is avoidance."

"It has worked so far."

"It will stop working."

He considered that in silence, which was also not a denial.

Alex took a step down from the overlook and turned, walking backward a few paces so she could face him. "Fine. Let's test possibilities."

"No."

"Yes."

"No."

She ignored him. "Arden Field."

"No."

"Arden Station."

"Absolutely not."

She pretended to think more deeply. "The Quiet Ground."

He gave her a look.

"That was actually not terrible," she said. "You reacted too quickly."

"It sounds like a retirement colony."

She laughed. "All right, fair point."

He bent to pick up his duffel again and started back toward the house. Alex fell into step beside him.

"What about Horizon House?" she tried.

"No."

"North Gate."

"No."

"Waypoint."

"No."

"You're not even considering these."

"I am considering them. Briefly."

"That is not consideration. That is summary dismissal."

"It's efficient."

She smiled to herself. "What would you call it?"

"Nothing."

"That answer is growing stale."

"It remains correct."

They reached the front steps. Bill climbed the first two while Alex stopped below him and turned one more time to look back over the estate.

The transport was nearly secured now. Sunlight had climbed higher. The air already held that midmorning clarity that made every edge sharper and every shadow more defined.

"It really is a good place," she said quietly.

Bill paused.

Then, in a tone simpler and more unguarded than most of what he said, he answered, "Yes."

She looked up at him.

There was nothing dramatic in the moment, but she felt its truth. For all his capability, all his discipline, all the strange roads that had shaped him, this place mattered to him. Not as a possession. As an anchor.

Alex nodded once. "Then maybe it doesn't need a grand name."

"No."

"But it might eventually need a useful one."

He accepted that with a slight tilt of his head.

It was the closest thing to progress she was likely to get today.

Bill reached for the entry panel by the door.

And then both of them heard it.

A distant sound at first.

Low.

Steady.

Approaching.

Not ground traffic.

A ship.

Bill stopped with his hand still near the panel and turned immediately toward the sky beyond the landing field.

Alex did the same.

The sound grew louder over the next few seconds, clean and controlled, not the wild rush of someone coming in too fast or off vector. This was a deliberate approach. Professional. Intentional.

A small transport crested the distant tree line and moved into view, sunlight flashing across its hull. It was not large, but it was not civilian local traffic either. The craft held its line with practiced precision as it descended toward the landing area Bill's own transport had only recently left clear.

Alex frowned. "Were you expecting someone?"

Bill's answer came without hesitation. "No."

That was enough to sharpen the moment.

Unexpected arrivals were rarely casual, especially now.

Together they moved back toward the overlook and watched as the incoming ship aligned over the field. Dust swirled in widening rings as the pilot brought it down. The landing was smooth. Too smooth to be improvised.

Whoever this was, they had come with purpose.

Ground crew who had only just finished with the earlier transport were already repositioning, alert but not alarmed. Bill said nothing, but Alex could feel his attention sharpen beside her. He had gone very still.

The new transport settled fully onto the field.

Its engines wound down.

For a few seconds nothing happened.

Then the hatch opened.

A single figure stepped out first—a man in a dark survey uniform with a light coat folded back at the sides, carrying no visible weapon and moving with the brisk focus of someone who did not intend to waste time. Another person remained just inside the hatch, likely crew.

The man scanned the field, spotted Bill and Alex on the rise, and immediately started toward them.

Alex folded her arms lightly. "That doesn't look social."

"No."

"You're full of warmth this morning."

Bill did not answer. His eyes remained on the approaching visitor.

The man crossed the lower section of the field at a quick but controlled pace, then moved onto the gravel path leading upward. By the time he reached the front steps, he was breathing a little harder from the climb, but his expression had not changed. He looked like someone holding himself together through concentration rather than ease.

He stopped a respectful distance away.

"Mr. Arden?"

Bill gave a short nod. "Yes."

The man glanced once at Alex, assessing, then back to Bill. "My name is Daniel Mercer. I'm with the Colonial Survey Authority."

There was no preamble in him. No politeness for its own sake. Only urgency held in check by discipline.

Bill waited.

Mercer continued. "I apologize for arriving unannounced, but we were told delay would be unwise."

Alex felt the air shift almost imperceptibly around the words.

Bill said, "What happened?"

Mercer drew in one measured breath.

"We have a situation on a survey world," he said. "An expedition team has gone missing."

He paused.

"And we were told," he finished, looking directly at Bill, "you might be able to help."

Bill's expression did not change.

But Alex, standing beside him, felt the quiet morning settle into something else entirely.

The calm of home was still there.

The open ground was still there.

The sun was still bright across the field.

But the next road had already arrived.

And it had brought a name with it.

Asterra-9.

Chapter 2 — Asterra-9

For a few seconds after Mercer spoke, no one moved.

The morning had not changed. The light still rested across the field. The wind still moved through the grass below the rise. Somewhere behind them, one of the ground crew called out a routine check and received a routine answer.

But the shape of the moment had shifted.

Bill studied the man in front of him—not in a confrontational way, not even in a suspicious one, but with the quiet precision of someone already sorting what mattered from what did not.

"Who told you that?" Bill asked.

Mercer seemed prepared for the question. "Director Halverson. Survey Authority central."

Bill gave a slight nod. He knew the name. Not personally, but enough to understand the weight behind it. Halverson was not someone who sent people across distance on a vague recommendation.

"What kind of situation?" Bill asked.

Mercer hesitated—not because he did not know the answer, but because he seemed to be choosing how much to say at once.

"A lost team," he said finally. "Full expedition unit. Survey, mapping, environmental verification. Standard operation."

"That doesn't usually require this kind of arrival," Alex said.

Mercer glanced at her again, briefly, then back to Bill. "No," he agreed. "It doesn't."

Bill said, “Start from the beginning.”

Mercer nodded once. “May we step inside?”

Bill turned toward the door and keyed the entry panel without another word.

The interior of the house carried the same tone as the exterior—clean, structured, functional without feeling cold. The main room opened into a broad space with long tables, integrated displays, and a wall-length window overlooking the land below. There were no unnecessary decorations, but there was nothing unfinished either. Everything had a place. Everything worked.

Mercer took it in quickly, then set a compact case on the table nearest the center of the room.

Alex moved to the far side, resting one hand lightly against the surface as she watched him. Bill remained standing near the end of the table, not leaning, not shifting—simply present.

Mercer opened the case and activated the projector inside.

A soft hum filled the room as a three-dimensional display formed above the table. A star field resolved first—clean points of light against a dark background—then a highlighted region appeared along the outer edge of mapped space.

“This is the sector,” Mercer said.

The display zoomed in smoothly.

A single world rotated into view.

“Asterra-9.”

The planet appeared calm at first glance. Blue-green surface. Broad continental shapes. No obvious atmospheric disturbances. No visible signs of violent weather patterns or geological instability.

Alex leaned in slightly. “That’s classified as low-risk?”

"Yes," Mercer said. "Very low. It's been surveyed twice before. Preliminary mapping confirmed stable terrain, breathable atmosphere, low predator index, minimal environmental hazards."

"Minimal," Alex repeated. "Not none."

"Nothing outside standard expedition parameters," Mercer said.

Bill was still watching the planet.

"How long ago was the last survey?" he asked.

"Eighteen months."

"And no issues reported?"

"None."

Bill's eyes shifted slightly, not leaving the display but changing focus.

"What changed?"

Mercer exhaled quietly. "That's what we're trying to understand."

He adjusted the projection.

A series of markers appeared across the planet's surface—small, evenly spaced points forming a loose grid across one of the major landmasses.

"This was the most recent expedition," Mercer said. "Pathfinder Dawn support team in orbit. Ground team of twelve. Their assignment was routine—refine mapping resolution, confirm resource indicators, and complete environmental consistency checks."

Alex's brow furrowed slightly. "Consistency checks?"

"Comparing current conditions to prior survey data," Mercer said. "Standard procedure before a world is upgraded from preliminary classification."

"Meaning?" she asked.

"Meaning before it's opened for broader use," he said. "Settlement planning. Resource allocation. Transit routing."

Alex nodded slowly.

Bill said, "When did they arrive?"

"Twenty-three days ago."

"And when did you lose them?"

Mercer's jaw tightened slightly. "Nine days ago."

The room seemed to settle around that number.

Nine days was long enough for something to be seriously wrong.

"What was the last transmission?" Bill asked.

Mercer tapped the case.

The projection shifted again, and a waveform appeared alongside a short audio file.

"Recovered from orbital relay," Mercer said. "Partial signal. There was interference."

He activated playback.

Static filled the room for a moment—thin, uneven, like something interfering with the transmission rather than simple distance loss.

Then a voice broke through.

"…adjusting position… grid doesn't—"

More static.

"…reading doesn't match—hold on—"

A sharp spike of distortion.

"…this isn't—"

The signal cut.

Silence returned to the room.

Alex felt a slight tension settle between her shoulders.

"That's it?" she asked.

"That's all that came through," Mercer said.

Bill said nothing.

His attention had narrowed, not to the words themselves but to something underneath them.

"The grid doesn't match," he said quietly.

Mercer nodded. "Yes."

Alex looked between them. "What does that mean, exactly?"

Mercer gestured to the map. "The team was operating on a mapped coordinate grid. Fixed positions. Known distances. Established landmarks."

"And something didn't line up," Alex said.

"Yes."

"That could be equipment error," she said.

"It could," Mercer agreed.

Bill spoke again. "What happened next?"

Mercer brought up another layer of data.

"Orbital support attempted contact," he said. "No response. They initiated standard recovery protocol—sent drones first."

A series of small icons appeared across the map, moving outward from a central point.

"The drones reported inconsistent data," Mercer continued. "Distance readings fluctuating. Position markers shifting without corresponding movement."

Alex frowned. "Shifting how?"

Mercer hesitated again, just slightly. "Without pattern."

Bill's gaze sharpened.

"Everything has a pattern," he said.

Mercer met his eyes. "We haven't found one."

Bill looked back at the projection.

"How many recovery attempts?" he asked.

"Three," Mercer said. "All unsuccessful."

"Losses?"

Mercer shook his head. "No confirmed casualties. But no confirmed survivors either."

"That's a careful answer," Alex said.

"It's the accurate one," Mercer replied.

She held his gaze for a moment, then nodded once.

Bill stepped closer to the table.

"Show me the terrain," he said.

Mercer adjusted the display again.

The planet's surface expanded into a detailed topographical map. Broad plains stretched across the region where the expedition had been working. Low elevation changes. Scattered rock formations. Sparse vegetation clusters. Nothing that would obstruct visibility for long distances.

"You can see for miles," Mercer said quietly. "There's nowhere to get lost."

Alex studied the map.

"Unless," she said, "something changes that."

Mercer did not respond.

Bill's eyes moved slowly across the terrain, taking in relationships rather than individual features.

"Where were they operating when the signal came through?" he asked.

Mercer highlighted a section of the grid.

"Here."

Bill leaned slightly closer.

"Zoom in."

The display responded.

Landmarks resolved—rock lines, elevation markers, environmental tags.

Everything looked ordinary.

Too ordinary.

Bill straightened.

"What about the maps?" he asked.

Mercer hesitated.

"That's one of the problems," he said.

"What problem?"

Mercer tapped another control.

A second map overlaid the first.

At a glance, they appeared identical.

At a second glance, they were not.

Lines did not align exactly. Markers sat slightly off from where they should have been. Distances between points were subtly different.

Alex leaned in. "That's… not a calibration error."

"No," Mercer said. "It isn't."

Bill studied the overlap in silence.

"How long between these two sets?" he asked.

"Six hours."

That was enough.

Alex felt it immediately.

"That shouldn't happen," she said.

"No," Mercer agreed.

Bill's expression remained unchanged, but something in him had settled.

"What did the team report before the transmission?" he asked.

Mercer brought up a final set of logs.

"Routine updates," he said. "Progress reports. Environmental confirmations. Nothing unusual."

Bill said, "Until it was."

Mercer nodded.

Alex folded her arms lightly, thinking.

"You said search teams failed," she said. "What exactly does that mean?"

Mercer answered carefully. "They couldn't locate the ground team."

"That's not the same as not finding them," she said.

"No."

"What did they find?"

Mercer's pause this time was longer.

"Tracks," he said.

"Tracks?"

"Foot movement. Equipment marks. Signs of recent activity."

Alex's eyes narrowed. "And?"

"And they didn't lead anywhere."

That hung in the air.

Bill looked at Mercer. "Explain."

Mercer met his gaze. "Paths would begin normally. Movement across terrain. Then… they would fade."

"Fade," Alex repeated.

"Yes."

"As in disappear?"

"Yes."

Alex shook her head slowly. "That's not possible."

Mercer did not argue.

Bill said, "What about aerial observation?"

"Visual confirmation only," Mercer said. "No anomalies detected from orbit."

"But on the ground," Bill said.

Mercer nodded once.

"Something doesn't match."

The room went quiet again.

Not uncertain this time.

Focused.

Alex looked at the map, then at the overlaid discrepancies, then back at Mercer.

"You said this world was stable," she said.

"It was," Mercer replied.

"That's past tense."

He didn't answer.

Bill turned slightly away from the table, looking out through the long window toward the open land beyond the house.

For a moment, Alex thought he might say nothing at all.

Then he asked, without turning back, "Why us?"

Mercer's answer came without hesitation this time.

"Because you don't rely on assumptions," he said. "Because you've handled situations where data didn't align with reality. And because the people still out there"—he paused—"may not have much time left."

That last part landed differently.

Alex felt it.

Bill did too.

He turned back to the table.

For a few seconds, he said nothing.

Then he asked one final question.

"Has anyone explained it?"

Mercer shook his head. "No."

Bill looked at the shifting overlay of maps.

The misaligned grid.
The inconsistent distances.
The tracks that led nowhere.

He reached out and deactivated the overlay, leaving only the clean image of the planet rotating slowly above the table.

Calm.
Orderly.
Untroubled.

It looked like any other survey world.

Bill studied it for another moment.

Then he said, simply, "We'll take a look."

Mercer let out a breath he had likely been holding since before he landed.

"Thank you," he said.

Alex glanced at Bill.

There was no hesitation in him now.

No uncertainty.

Just direction.

She turned back to the projection.

Asterra-9 rotated quietly in the air between them.

A stable world.
A mapped world.
A world where nothing should have gone wrong.

And yet it had.

Alex folded her arms again, more thoughtfully this time.

"Then we should plan to leave soon," she said.

Bill nodded once.

"Yes."

Outside, the wind moved across the field, unchanged.

But inside, the next mission had already begun.

Chapter 3 — Descent

Preparation did not take long.

That, Alex noticed, was not because there was little to do—but because Bill did not allow unnecessary delay to form around important decisions. Once he had said *yes*, the work moved forward without hesitation or announcement. There were no formal declarations, no drawn-out planning sessions for their own sake. Just motion.

Within an hour, the house had shifted from quiet return to controlled activity.

Equipment cases were opened and checked. Portable scanners were calibrated and rechecked against baseline standards. Field packs were assembled with deliberate efficiency—nothing excessive, nothing missing. Communications units were tested across multiple bands. Alex reviewed environmental data while cross-referencing known anomalies, even though Mercer had already confirmed that none had been recorded.

Still, she checked again.

Because something *had* gone wrong.

And she did not intend to walk into it unprepared.

Bill moved through the process without commentary. He did not rush. He did not repeat work. He simply progressed from one task to the next as though the sequence had already been arranged somewhere in his mind before his hands ever touched the equipment.

At one point, Alex watched him reassemble a compact navigation unit after running a diagnostic on its internal alignment systems.

"You don't trust their data," she said.

"I trust that something changed," Bill replied.

"That's not the same thing."

"No."

She leaned back slightly against the table. "So we verify everything ourselves."

"Yes."

Alex nodded. That matched her thinking.

Mercer remained nearby, speaking occasionally with Survey Authority command through a secure channel. His tone had shifted since their decision. Less urgency now, more structure. The moment of asking had passed. Now they were in the phase where things either went right—or didn't.

"Transport is ready when you are," Mercer said at last, closing the channel.

Bill secured the final case and stood. "We're ready."

Alex glanced once more at the equipment spread across the table—then at Bill.

He gave a small nod.

That was enough.

The shuttle Mercer had arrived in was already prepped for departure when they reached the landing field.

It was not large, but it was well-maintained. Survey Authority markings ran along the side in clean lines. The hull showed signs of use—light scarring, minor surface wear—but nothing neglected. This was a working craft, not a ceremonial one.

The pilot stood just outside the open hatch, reviewing a checklist on a handheld unit. He looked up as they approached.

"Mr. Arden," he said with a respectful nod. "Ma'am."

"Status?" Bill asked.

"Flight systems green," the pilot replied. "Navigation locked to orbital relay. Estimated transit time to Asterra-9—nine days."

Alex glanced sideways at Bill.

There it was.

Not down the block.

Nine days.

Bill gave no reaction outwardly, but she knew he had already accounted for it.

"Any issues with the route?" Bill asked.

"Nothing significant," the pilot said. "Standard corridor. We'll have minor drift adjustments near the outer range, but nothing outside normal parameters."

Bill nodded once. "Good."

The pilot stepped aside. "Whenever you're ready."

They boarded without ceremony.

The interior of the shuttle was compact but comfortable enough for extended travel. Seating was arranged along the sides with a central aisle leading forward to the cockpit. Equipment racks lined the rear section, already secured for transit. A small operations console had been set up midway along the cabin, allowing for data review and communication without entering the cockpit.

Alex took a seat near the console.

Bill sat across from her.

Mercer remained standing for a moment, then moved toward the forward section to coordinate final departure clearance.

The hatch sealed with a soft, solid sound.

For a brief moment, everything was still.

Then the engines engaged.

A low vibration ran through the structure—not harsh, not disruptive, but present. A reminder that motion had begun.

Alex exhaled slowly.

"Here we go," she said.

Bill gave a slight nod.

The ascent was smooth.

The shuttle lifted cleanly from the field, rising above the estate in a controlled arc. Through the side viewport, Alex watched the land fall away—the buildings shrinking, the landing field becoming a simple shape against the green below, the roads turning into faint lines that curved through open ground.

For a moment, she felt the familiar pull of perspective.

How quickly something that had felt immediate could become distant.

Bill watched as well, though she could not tell exactly what he was thinking. With him, that was often the case. His focus moved through layers that did not always show on the surface.

The shuttle cleared the lower atmosphere within minutes.

Blue shifted to black.

The curve of the planet revealed itself in full—wide, silent, and indifferent to whatever concerns occupied the people leaving it behind.

Alex rested her arm lightly against the window frame.

"You ever notice," she said, "that no matter how many times you leave a planet, it always feels like something is being left unfinished?"

Bill considered that.

"Yes."

"Even when you know you'll be back."

"Yes."

She nodded once. "Good. I thought that might just be me."

"It isn't."

They sat in quiet for a moment as the shuttle transitioned fully into space.

Ahead, the stars stretched out in sharp, unmoving clarity.

"Course set," the pilot's voice came from the forward cabin. "Engaging long-range transit."

The engines shifted tone—deeper now, steadier.

Alex felt the change more than she heard it.

The journey had truly begun.

The first hours passed in practical work.

Alex reviewed mission data again, this time with the knowledge that they would soon be relying on it directly. She cross-checked environmental readings, terrain reports, and prior survey logs. Everything confirmed the same conclusion.

Asterra-9 should have been safe.

That was the problem.

She glanced up at Bill.

He was not looking at the data display.

He was looking at nothing.

Or rather—he was looking *through* everything.

"You're building something," she said.

He shifted his gaze slightly. "Yes."

"A model."

"Yes."

"Based on incomplete information."

"Yes."

She leaned back. "That seems risky."

"It is."

"Comforting."

He almost smiled.

By the second day, routine began to form.

Meals were simple and timed more by necessity than schedule. Sleep came in measured cycles. The pilot maintained steady progress along the designated corridor, making occasional adjustments as minor drift variations required.

Alex found herself falling into a rhythm she recognized from previous missions—but this one felt different.

Not because of the work.

Because of the unknown.

On Havenfall, the problem had been visible. Difficult, dangerous, complex—but visible. There had been something to push against.

Here, the problem was absence.

Missing people.

Shifting data.

A map that no longer matched the ground.

That kind of problem had edges that were harder to define.

And that made it harder to solve.

"Walk me through it," Alex said on the third day.

Bill looked up from where he had been reviewing a stripped-down version of the terrain model—one with most of the instrument overlays removed.

"What part?" he asked.

"What you think is happening."

He considered that.

Then he said, "Something is affecting spatial consistency."

"That's a careful way of saying things don't line up."

"Yes."

"How?" she asked.

He tapped the display once.

Two points appeared.

"Distance between these points should be fixed," he said.

"Yes."

"It isn't."

"That suggests measurement error."

"Yes."

"But you don't think it is."

"No."

"Why?"

Bill shifted slightly, choosing his words.

"Because the inconsistency is reported from multiple sources," he said. "Independent systems. Different methods."

"So not just a faulty instrument."

"No."

Alex folded her arms lightly. "Then what?"

Bill looked back at the simplified terrain.

"The relationship between positions is changing," he said.

She watched him carefully.

"That's not a small problem," she said.

"No."

"That's a fundamental problem."

"Yes."

Alex let that sit for a moment.

"If that's true," she said slowly, "then the team didn't get lost."

Bill met her eyes.

"They couldn't find where they were."

That landed.

Harder than she expected.

By the fifth day, even Mercer had grown quieter.

He still communicated regularly with Survey Authority, still logged updates, still reviewed incoming data—but the edge of urgency had settled into something else.

Concern.

Measured, controlled, but present.

At one point he approached where Bill and Alex were seated.

"Orbital team confirms no additional signals," he said. "No new transmissions from the surface."

Bill nodded once.

Mercer hesitated. "We're still within expected survival window," he added.

Alex looked at him. "That's an optimistic interpretation."

"It's an accurate one," Mercer said.

Bill said nothing.

Mercer studied him for a moment, then said, "You've seen situations like this before?"

"Not this one," Bill replied.

"That's not what I asked."

Bill met his gaze.

"I've seen situations where what should be true… isn't," he said.

Mercer nodded slowly.

"That's what we're dealing with," he said.

"Yes."

By the seventh day, anticipation had replaced routine.

There was nothing more to prepare.

Nothing more to refine.

Only arrival remained.

Alex stood near the forward viewport, watching the distant starfield shift almost imperceptibly as the shuttle adjusted its approach vector.

"You ever think about how strange this is?" she said.

Bill looked over.

"We're heading toward a world that looks normal," she continued, "that has no recorded hazards, no environmental threats, no visible danger… and yet an entire team disappeared on it."

"Yes."

"That should bother me more than it does."

"It does bother you."

She considered that. "Yes," she admitted. "It does."

On the ninth day, Asterra-9 came into view.

At first, it was only a point of light—indistinguishable from the stars around it.

Then it grew.

Slowly.

Deliberately.

Until it resolved into shape.

A world.

Blue-green.

Calm.

Beautiful, in the quiet way untroubled planets often are.

Alex stared at it through the viewport.

"There's nothing wrong with it," she said.

Bill stood beside her.

"No," he said.

"There's nowhere to hide," she added. "No dense forest, no deep canyon systems, no atmospheric distortions."

"No."

"And yet—"

"Yes."

She exhaled slowly.

"That's the problem."

"Entering orbital range," the pilot announced. "Pathfinder Dawn is holding position above the primary survey zone."

The shuttle adjusted its trajectory.

As they drew closer, a second shape came into view—a station in orbit.

Clean.

Functional.

Watching.

Alex felt the tension return, quiet but unmistakable.

"Here we go," she said again, more softly this time.

Bill didn't answer.

He was already focused on the world below.

The shuttle eased into orbital alignment.

Below them, Asterra-9 stretched wide and open.

Unchanged.

Untroubled.

As though nothing had happened at all.

And that, Alex realized, was the most unsettling part.

"Welcome to Asterra-9," Mercer said quietly.

No one responded.

Because whatever waited below them…

…was not visible from here.

Chapter 4 — Ground That Doesn't Match

The shuttle's descent began with a subtle shift.

Not dramatic. Not urgent. Just a gradual change in motion that pressed lightly against the body and signaled that space was giving way to atmosphere. The stars outside the viewport softened, then disappeared as the upper layers of Asterra-9's atmosphere wrapped around the hull in a faint shimmer.

Alex watched the transition closely.

There was nothing unusual in it.

No turbulence beyond normal variation. No electrical interference. No visible anomalies. The readouts scrolling across the console remained clean, stable, reassuring in the way well-behaved systems tend to be.

If she had seen this descent without context, she would have marked it as routine.

That thought stayed with her.

"Entry profile is nominal," the pilot reported. "No atmospheric disturbance. Guidance systems stable."

Bill stood behind the forward console, one hand resting lightly against the frame. He wasn't watching the instruments.

He was watching the horizon.

Cloud layers passed beneath them—thin, scattered formations that broke easily as the shuttle moved through. Beyond them, the surface of Asterra-9 came into clearer view.

Wide plains.

Low, rolling variations in terrain.

Long lines of rock formations that cast narrow shadows in the angled light.

Nothing dense enough to obscure visibility for long distances.

Nothing complex enough to confuse direction.

"You can see for miles," Alex said quietly.

Mercer, standing near the cockpit entrance, nodded. "That's what the first survey teams reported."

"And the second," Alex added.

"Yes."

She leaned slightly closer to the viewport.

"There's nowhere to get lost," she said.

Bill didn't respond.

"Landing coordinates confirmed," the pilot said. "We'll be touching down near the original survey grid."

The shuttle adjusted its descent path.

As they dropped lower, details sharpened.

What had been general shapes became specific features—rock ridges, shallow depressions, sparse clusters of low vegetation that broke up the otherwise open terrain. The color of the ground shifted subtly with elevation and composition, but the overall impression remained the same.

Open.

Navigable.

Clear.

Alex felt the contradiction settle more firmly in her thoughts.

"Any visual markers from orbit?" she asked.

Mercer shook his head. "None that indicated distress or disruption."

"No crash sites. No signal flares. No structural damage."

"No."

She exhaled slowly. "That's consistent with the reports."

"It is."

"And still doesn't explain anything."

"No."

The shuttle touched down with a soft, controlled impact.

Engines eased back.

For a moment, everything was still.

Alex felt the familiar pause again—the one that comes at the threshold between preparation and reality.

Then the hatch released.

The first thing she noticed was the silence.

Not the absence of sound entirely—there was wind, faint but present, moving across the open land—but the lack of anything else.

No mechanical noise.

No distant activity.

No indication that anyone had been here recently.

She stepped down onto the surface.

The ground felt firm beneath her boots.

Not loose. Not unstable.

Solid.

Bill followed.

Mercer and the pilot remained near the shuttle for a moment, completing post-landing checks before joining them.

Alex turned slowly, taking in the surrounding terrain.

From ground level, the openness was even more pronounced.

The horizon stretched wide in every direction, broken only by distant rock formations and subtle elevation changes. The sky above was clear, the light steady and clean. Visibility extended far enough that anything moving across the surface should have been seen well in advance.

She said it again, almost to herself.

"There's nowhere to get lost."

Bill stepped forward a few paces, scanning the terrain without speaking.

He didn't look at everything.

He looked at relationships.

Alex had begun to recognize that difference.

Mercer approached from behind them. "The expedition established their primary base approximately two kilometers from here."

Alex glanced at him. "Why not land directly there?"

"Because we don't know what we're landing into," Mercer said.

That was fair.

Bill said, "Show me the direction."

Mercer activated a handheld unit and projected a simple directional marker into the air.

"North-northeast," he said. "Straight line."

Bill looked at the horizon, then back at the marker.

Then he started walking.

Alex followed immediately.

At first, everything behaved exactly as expected.

Their pace was steady.

The terrain underfoot remained consistent.

Landmarks approached at a predictable rate.

Alex kept one eye on the handheld unit, comparing their movement against the projected grid.

"Distance tracking normal," she said after a minute.

Bill didn't respond.

They passed a low ridge of rock—nothing large, just a natural formation that rose slightly above the surrounding ground. Beyond it, the land opened again into another stretch of wide, uninterrupted terrain.

Alex marked the ridge mentally.

A reference point.

She checked the unit again.

"Still on track," she said.

Mercer nodded. "This matches the initial survey logs."

They continued.

After several minutes, Alex looked up again.

The next landmark—a distinct, narrow rock formation that stood slightly apart from the others—should have been closer.

She frowned.

"How far out is that formation?" she asked.

Mercer checked his unit. "Approximately eight hundred meters."

Alex looked at it again.

It didn't feel like eight hundred meters.

She didn't say that out loud.

Instead, she said, "We should be halfway there by now."

Mercer checked again. "We are."

Alex slowed slightly.

She looked from the formation… to the ground beneath her feet… then back again.

Something didn't align.

Not clearly.

Not dramatically.

Just enough to unsettle her sense of distance.

Bill stopped.

Alex noticed immediately.

"What is it?" she asked.

He didn't answer right away.

He was looking at the formation.

Then he looked down.

Then back again.

"It's taking too long," he said.

Mercer glanced at his unit. "Our speed is consistent."

Bill nodded once. "Yes."

Alex felt it click.

"We're moving normally," she said slowly.

"Yes," Bill replied.

"But the distance isn't closing the way it should."

"Yes."

Mercer looked between them. "That could be perception."

Alex shook her head. "No."

She turned slightly, looking back toward the ridge they had passed.

It looked… farther away than it should have been.

Not dramatically.

Just enough.

She checked the unit again.

The numbers said everything was correct.

Her eyes said something else.

"Let's verify," Alex said.

She picked a point on the ground and marked it with a small beacon from her pack.

"From here to that formation," she said, "we walk a measured distance. Then we check."

Bill nodded.

They moved forward again.

Alex counted her steps.

Carefully.

Consistently.

When she reached the expected count, she stopped.

The formation was still farther away than it should have been.

She turned slowly.

The beacon behind them looked closer than it should have been.

Her stomach tightened slightly.

"That's not right," she said.

Mercer checked his unit again, more quickly this time.

"Distance readings are stable," he said.

"They're wrong," Alex replied.

"They're consistent."

"That doesn't make them right."

Bill walked a few steps forward, then stopped again.

He wasn't looking at the unit.

He wasn't looking at the formation directly.

He was looking at the space between them.

As though trying to see something that wasn't visible.

Alex watched him.

"What do you see?" she asked.

He didn't answer.

Not immediately.

Then he said, "It's not distance."

Alex frowned. "Then what is it?"

Bill turned slightly, looking at the ridge behind them, then the formation ahead, then back again.

"It's alignment," he said.

Mercer's expression tightened. "Explain."

Bill shook his head once. "Not yet."

A faint crackle sounded over Alex's comm unit.

She turned her head slightly.

"Say again?" she said.

Only static answered.

Then, faintly, an echo.

Not a clear transmission.

Just a fragment of sound repeating itself with a slight delay.

Alex lowered the unit.

"That shouldn't happen," she said.

Mercer checked his own. "Signal integrity is stable."

"It's not," Alex said. "I just heard—"

The echo came again.

Softer this time.

Almost like a reflection of a sound that hadn't fully formed.

Bill looked at her.

"What did you hear?" he asked.

She hesitated.

"I'm not sure," she admitted. "It sounded like… us. But delayed."

Mercer frowned. "That's not possible under current conditions."

Alex didn't argue.

She simply looked back toward the formation.

It still hadn't moved the way it should have.

"Recalibrate," Mercer said, more to himself than anyone else.

He adjusted the settings on his unit, running a quick diagnostic.

"Systems are functioning," he said after a moment.

"Then the system is wrong," Alex replied.

Bill took another step forward.

Then another.

Then he stopped again.

Alex could see it now in the way he moved.

He wasn't walking *toward* something.

He was testing the space itself.

"We're not where we think we are," he said.

Mercer looked up sharply. "Our coordinates are fixed."

"No," Bill said quietly. "They aren't."

Alex felt the weight of that settle in.

She looked at the ground.

At her own footprints.

At the formation ahead.

At the ridge behind them.

Everything looked right.

And yet—

"It doesn't match," she said.

The wind moved across the open land.

The sky remained clear.

The terrain stretched out exactly as it should.

But something—something small, subtle, and deeply wrong—had already begun to show itself.

And now that she had seen it…

Alex knew she wouldn't be able to ignore it again.

Bill turned slightly, scanning the horizon once more.

Then he said, almost to himself—

"This is where it starts."

No one argued.

Because they all knew—

Something on Asterra-9 did not behave the way it should.

And they had only just stepped into it.

Chapter 5 — The Edge of Understanding

They did not turn back.

That, Alex realized later, was not a decision that had been discussed.

It simply… hadn't come up.

Once the inconsistency had revealed itself—once the distance no longer behaved the way distance should—there was no clean line that said *this is the point where we stop.* There was only the quiet understanding that whatever had happened to the missing team had begun somewhere ahead of them.

And if they were going to find answers—

They had to move forward.

"Mark this location," Alex said.

She crouched briefly and placed another beacon on the ground. The device activated with a soft pulse of light—steady, reliable, anchored.

At least, it was supposed to be.

Mercer logged the coordinates automatically. "Marker one confirmed."

Alex stood and looked ahead again.

The narrow rock formation was still there.

Still the same distance.

Still wrong.

"Let's continue," Bill said.

No one argued.

They adjusted their approach.

Instead of walking in a straight line, Bill shifted slightly to the left, angling their path across the terrain rather than directly toward the formation.

Alex noticed immediately.

"You're not heading for it," she said.

"No."

"Why?"

Bill glanced ahead. "I want to see what changes."

That made sense.

If the problem was alignment—not distance—then direction might matter more than speed.

They moved.

At first, nothing changed.

The ground remained firm.

The wind remained steady.

The horizon remained clear.

Alex kept one eye on the beacon behind them.

It should have grown smaller at a predictable rate.

It didn't.

It lingered.

As though it were reluctant to let go of its position relative to them.

She didn't like that thought.

"Signal check," Mercer said.

Alex tapped her comm unit. "Reading you."

"Reading you," Mercer confirmed.

Bill gave a short nod.

For a moment, everything seemed stable.

Then—

"…reading you…"

The echo returned.

Faint.

Delayed.

Alex froze slightly.

"You heard that?" she asked.

Mercer's expression tightened. "Yes."

Bill said nothing.

But Alex saw his attention sharpen again.

They continued moving.

This time, Alex paid closer attention to the terrain itself.

Not just where they were going—

But how the space behaved around them.

She picked another landmark—a low cluster of rocks off to their right.

It should have passed behind them within a minute.

It didn't.

Instead, it seemed to drift.

Not with them.

Not away from them.

Just… *off.*

Like a reference point that had slipped slightly out of place.

Alex slowed.

"Do you see that?" she asked.

Mercer followed her gaze. "Yes."

"That's not tracking correctly."

"No."

Bill stopped.

Again.

He turned in a slow circle—not quickly, not searching, but *measuring.*

Alex watched him.

"What are you looking for?" she asked.

He didn't answer right away.

Then he said, "Consistency."

Mercer let out a quiet breath. "You're not going to find it."

Bill's expression didn't change. "Everything has it."

"Not this," Mercer said.

Bill looked at him.

Then, calmly, "Yes. This too."

They reached a point where the terrain dipped slightly.

Not a valley—just a shallow depression that altered the angle of the ground for a short distance before leveling out again.

Bill stepped down into it.

Alex followed.

The moment she did—

Something shifted.

Not visibly.

Not dramatically.

But *felt.*

She stopped mid-step.

"What was that?" she said.

Mercer looked at her. "What?"

"I don't know," she said, frowning. "It felt like—"

She searched for the word.

"—like stepping onto something that isn't where it should be."

Mercer glanced down at the ground. "It's solid."

"I know it's solid," Alex said. "That's not what I meant."

Bill was standing still now, just ahead of them.

"Stay there," he said.

Alex froze.

Mercer did the same.

Bill took one slow step forward.

Then another.

Then he stopped.

He turned slightly.

"Now come forward," he said.

Alex stepped toward him.

The moment she crossed the same point—

The feeling returned.

Stronger this time.

A subtle disorientation.

Not enough to make her stumble.

But enough to make her question her own position.

She stopped beside him.

"That's it," she said quietly.

Mercer moved next.

When he reached them, he paused as well.

"I felt that," he admitted.

Bill looked back toward the direction they had come from.

Then forward again.

Then down.

"It's not uniform," he said.

Alex nodded slowly. "No."

"Localized variations," Mercer added.

Bill shook his head slightly. "Not exactly."

Alex looked at him. "Then what?"

Bill didn't answer.

Not yet.

"Let's test it," Alex said.

She took a small marker from her pack and placed it on the ground at the edge of the depression.

"Reference point," she said.

Then she stepped back.

"From here to there," she said, pointing to a point several meters ahead, "we move in a straight line."

Bill nodded.

They moved.

Carefully.

Step by step.

Alex kept her eyes fixed on the marker behind them.

At first, it behaved normally.

Then—

It didn't.

It shifted.

Not positionally.

Relationally.

The angle felt wrong.

The distance felt compressed—

Then extended—

Then neither.

Alex stopped abruptly.

"No," she said.

Mercer looked at his unit again. "Distance is stable."

"It's not," Alex said firmly.

Bill turned.

He walked back toward the marker.

Alex watched closely.

As he moved—

The space around him seemed to… hesitate.

Not visibly.

But perceptibly.

When he reached the marker, he crouched briefly, studying it.

Then he stood and walked back toward them.

When he reached Alex, he said, "It's not the ground."

She frowned. "Then what is it?"

Bill looked at her.

Then at Mercer.

Then at the horizon.

"It's the relationship between positions," he said.

Mercer exhaled slowly. "You've said that before."

Bill nodded. "Yes."

"And now?"

"Now we're inside it."

A sudden tone sounded over Mercer's unit.

He looked down quickly.

"Signal," he said.

Alex turned. "From where?"

Mercer adjusted the display. "Surface transmission. Weak."

"Lock it," Bill said.

Mercer worked quickly.

"Got it," he said. "But it's unstable."

"Play it."

The audio came through in fragments.

"…anyone—"

Static.

"…can't hold—"

More static.

"…position isn't—"

The signal shifted.

Faded.

Then returned—

"…please—"

It cut again.

Alex felt her chest tighten.

"That's recent," she said.

"Yes," Mercer replied.

Bill looked toward the horizon.

"Direction," he said.

Mercer checked the signal vector.

"It doesn't hold," he said. "It's shifting."

Bill nodded once.

"Then we don't follow the signal," he said.

Alex looked at him. "Then what do we follow?"

Bill's eyes moved slowly across the terrain.

"We follow what doesn't change," he said.

Alex almost laughed.

"Nothing here isn't changing."

Bill met her gaze.

"Yes," he said.

"That's the problem."

A new sound interrupted them.

Low.

Controlled.

Descending.

Alex turned sharply toward the sky.

A ship.

Not theirs.

Not the shuttle they had arrived in.

This one approached with precision—clean lines, controlled descent, no hesitation in its movement.

Mercer looked up. "That's not Survey Authority."

Bill didn't respond.

He was already watching.

The ship lowered steadily toward a position not far from their landing site.

It touched down smoothly.

Engines powered down.

Silence returned.

For a moment, no one spoke.

Then the hatch opened.

A figure stepped out.

Then another.

Professional movement.

Deliberate.

Measured.

Alex felt the shift before anyone said it.

"This just changed," she said.

Bill nodded once.

"Yes."

They watched as the new arrivals began moving toward them across the open terrain.

Their pace was steady.

Confident.

Unhurried.

As though they already understood something the others did not.

Mercer's voice was lower now. "Who are they?"

Bill didn't take his eyes off them.

"Someone who's been watching this longer than we have," he said.

The lead figure reached them first.

A man.

Mid-40s, perhaps.

Composed.

Focused.

He stopped at a respectful distance.

His gaze moved from Mercer…

…to Alex…

…and finally to Bill.

There was recognition there.

Not surprise.

Not curiosity.

Recognition.

"My name is Elias Varn," he said.

His voice was calm.

Controlled.

"You've stepped into something that isn't behaving the way you expect."

Alex almost smiled at that.

"That's one way to put it," she said.

Varn didn't look at her.

He was still watching Bill.

"We've been monitoring this region," he said.

Bill's response was simple.

"For how long?"

Varn paused.

Then—

"Long enough to know this isn't an accident."

The wind moved again across the open land.

The sky remained clear.

The terrain remained unchanged.

But the understanding of it—

That had just shifted.

And Alex knew, standing there between two teams looking at the same impossible ground—

They were no longer just searching for people.

They were standing at the edge of something much larger.

And they still didn't understand it.

Chapter 6 — The First Rescue

For a moment after Varn spoke, no one answered.

Not because there was nothing to say—but because whatever *this* was had just grown larger.

Not a simple search.

Not a mapping error.

Not a failed expedition.

Something deeper.

Something already known—at least in part—to the people now standing in front of them.

Alex studied Varn more carefully.

He didn't carry himself like Survey Authority.

Less procedural.

More… contained.

Like someone who had already decided what mattered and had no interest in explaining the rest unless necessary.

"Monitoring," Mercer said, picking up the thread. "You didn't report that."

Varn glanced at him briefly. "We don't report everything."

"That's not how this works," Mercer said.

"No," Varn agreed. "It isn't."

There was no argument in his tone.

Which somehow made it worse.

Bill stepped forward slightly.

Not aggressively.

Just enough to take control of the conversation without announcing it.

"What have you seen?" he asked.

Varn looked at him.

Measured him.

Then said, "Instability."

"That's not specific," Alex said.

"It's accurate," Varn replied.

She held his gaze. "So is 'unhelpful.'"

For the first time, something almost like acknowledgment crossed his expression.

Then he said, "Spatial relationships are shifting."

Bill nodded once.

"We've seen that," he said.

"Not fully," Varn replied.

Bill didn't react outwardly.

But Alex knew he had registered that.

Before either of them could respond—

Mercer's unit sounded again.

Sharper this time.

More urgent.

"Signal," Mercer said quickly.

Alex turned. "Same source?"

Mercer shook his head. "Stronger."

Bill was already moving.

"Direction," he said.

Mercer adjusted the display. "North—slightly east—but it's—"

"Shifting," Alex finished.

"Yes."

Bill didn't wait.

He started forward.

"Hold position," Varn said sharply.

Bill didn't stop.

Alex followed him immediately.

Mercer hesitated—then followed as well.

Behind them, Varn and his team exchanged a quick look.

Then they moved too.

The terrain ahead stretched open and clear.

No obstacles.

No cover.

Nothing to block movement.

And yet—

Alex could feel it now.

The subtle misalignment.

The way distance didn't behave quite right.

The way direction felt… negotiable.

"Keep visual references," she said quickly. "Don't rely on instruments."

Bill didn't respond.

But his movement adjusted slightly—anchoring to visible landmarks rather than the path Mercer's unit suggested.

"Signal strengthening," Mercer said. "But I can't hold a fixed point."

"Don't try," Bill said.

Mercer frowned. "Then how do we—"

"We don't chase it," Bill said. "We intercept it."

Alex glanced at him.

That made sense.

If the signal wasn't stable—

Then movement toward it had to be based on something else.

"There," Bill said suddenly.

Alex followed his gaze.

At first, she saw nothing.

Then—

Movement.

Faint.

Off to the right.

"Someone's out there," she said.

Mercer squinted. "I don't have visual."

Bill was already changing direction.

Not toward where the signal indicated—

Toward where he *saw*.

"Stay on me," he said.

Alex didn't hesitate.

She adjusted her path immediately, aligning with his position.

Mercer followed, though less confidently.

Behind them, Varn's team spread slightly, watching carefully.

The figure ahead became clearer.

A person.

Moving.

But not steadily.

Stopping.

Turning.

As though unsure of direction.

"Jonas," Mercer said under his breath.

"You recognize him?" Alex asked.

"Yes. Ground team engineer."

Bill didn't slow.

"Jonas!" Mercer called out.

The figure stopped.

Turned.

Looked directly at them.

For a moment, Alex felt relief—

They had him.

Then—

He turned away.

And walked in the opposite direction.

"What is he doing?" Mercer said.

"He's not seeing us where we are," Bill replied.

"Jonas!" Alex called.

The man stopped again.

Turned slightly.

But not toward them.

Toward a point… offset.

Like his perception of their position was shifted.

"His alignment is off," Bill said.

Alex nodded. "He's not where he thinks he is."

"Or we aren't," Mercer said.

"Stop," Bill said.

Everyone froze.

He stepped forward alone.

Slowly.

Carefully.

Not directly toward Jonas—

But at an angle.

Adjusting with each step.

Watching.

Measuring.

Alex held her breath.

"Jonas," Bill said.

Not loudly.

Not sharply.

Just enough.

The man turned again.

This time—

Closer.

Not perfectly aligned.

But closer.

Bill took another step.

Then another.

Each one deliberate.

Each one adjusted.

Alex could see it now—

He wasn't walking toward Jonas.

He was walking toward where Jonas *would be* if the space between them aligned correctly.

"Stay there," Bill said.

Jonas didn't respond.

But he stopped moving.

That was enough.

Bill closed the remaining distance.

The last few steps—

Were the hardest.

Alex could see it in the way he moved.

The slight hesitation.

The correction.

The way his footing adjusted as though the ground itself wasn't fully cooperating.

Then—

He reached him.

His hand closed around Jonas's arm.

And for a moment—

Everything stuttered.

Not visibly.

But perceptibly.

Like something resisted the contact.

Then—

It resolved.

Jonas staggered.

Blinking.

Disoriented.

"What—" he said. "Where—"

Bill steadied him.

"You're here," he said.

Jonas looked around.

Confusion flooding his expression.

"I couldn't find—" he said. "I was right—I was just—"

He stopped.

Because now—

He could see them.

Clearly.

Alex exhaled.

She hadn't realized she'd been holding her breath.

Mercer moved forward quickly.

"Jonas," he said. "Can you hear me?"

Jonas nodded slowly. "Yes."

"Where were you?"

Jonas looked at him.

Then at Bill.

"I don't know," he said.

Bill released his grip slowly—but stayed close.

Watching.

Measuring.

Ensuring.

Jonas remained stable.

Present.

Aligned.

"How did you find me?" Jonas asked.

Bill looked at him.

Simple.

Direct.

"You weren't where you thought you were," he said.

Behind them, Varn stepped closer.

His expression had changed.

Not dramatically.

But enough.

Recognition.

Not of Bill—

But of what Bill had just done.

Alex turned slightly, looking back across the terrain.

It hadn't changed.

Still open.

Still clear.

Still calm.

And yet—

They had just pulled someone out of it.

Not from a hidden place.

Not from a distance.

From a misalignment.

"This isn't just a search," she said quietly.

No one argued.

Because now—

They all understood.

The missing weren't simply lost.

They were slipping.

Out of position.

Out of alignment.

Out of reach.

And Bill—

Was the only one who had just proven he could reach them.

Varn spoke again.

Softer this time.

More certain.

"This is worse than we thought," he said.

Bill didn't look at him.

He was still watching Jonas.

Still confirming.

Still anchoring.

Alex looked at the open world around them.

Then back at Bill.

And for the first time since they had arrived—

She felt it clearly.

This wasn't just something he could help with.

This was something only he might be able to solve.

The wind moved again across Asterra-9.

Unchanged.

Untroubled.

As though none of this mattered at all.

But Alex knew better now.

And so did everyone else.

Because this wasn't just a world where people had gone missing.

This was a world where reality itself—

Didn't stay where it belonged.

Chapter 7 — Patterns That Don't Exist

They did not move immediately after the rescue.

No one said it out loud, but they all felt it—

The need to stop.

To confirm.

To understand what had just happened before stepping deeper into it.

Jonas stood a few paces from Bill, breathing steadily now, though his eyes still moved more than they should—tracking the space around him as if it might shift again if he looked away for too long.

Alex watched him carefully.

"Stay still," she said. "Just for a moment."

Jonas nodded. "I'm not going anywhere."

There was something in the way he said it that made Alex glance at Bill.

Not confidence.

Relief.

The kind that came from no longer being somewhere else.

Mercer moved closer, running a quick scan across Jonas with a handheld unit.

"Vitals are stable," he said. "No major anomalies."

Jonas let out a breath. "That's good to hear."

Mercer looked at him. "What do you remember?"

Jonas hesitated.

Then shook his head.

"I was following the grid," he said. "Standard pathing. Everything was normal."

Alex listened closely.

"Then what changed?" she asked.

Jonas frowned. "Nothing. That's the problem. Nothing *felt* different."

He looked down at his hands.

"I just couldn't… match anything anymore," he said. "The markers didn't line up. The distances felt wrong. I thought it was equipment."

"It wasn't," Alex said quietly.

Jonas looked at her.

"No," he said. "It wasn't."

Bill hadn't moved far.

He stood where he had been when he brought Jonas back—watching, not just the man, but the space around him.

Alex recognized that look now.

He wasn't done.

Not with this.

"What are you seeing?" she asked.

Bill didn't answer immediately.

Instead, he walked a slow circle around the point where he had made contact with Jonas.

Alex followed his movement with her eyes.

"What are you checking?" Mercer asked.

Bill stopped.

"The path," he said.

Mercer frowned. "We already know the path doesn't hold."

Bill shook his head slightly. "Not the path we walked."

Alex stepped closer. "Then what?"

Bill looked at the ground.

Then outward.

Then back again.

"The path we didn't walk," he said.

Alex blinked.

"That's not a sentence that explains anything," she said.

Bill nodded once. "Not yet."

He moved again.

This time more deliberately.

He walked several steps in the direction they had come from—then stopped.

Turned slightly.

Adjusted.

Moved again.

Alex watched carefully.

"What are you doing?" she asked.

"Rebuilding it," Bill said.

"Rebuilding what?"

"The movement."

Mercer shook his head. "We already have movement logs."

Bill didn't look at him.

"They're wrong," he said.

Mercer exhaled sharply. "They're consistent."

"That doesn't make them right," Alex said.

Mercer glanced at her.

Then back at Bill.

Then said nothing.

Bill continued.

Step.

Pause.

Adjust.

Step.

It wasn't random.

Alex could see that.

He was mapping something.

Not on the unit.

In his head.

"Come here," Bill said.

Alex moved to his side immediately.

"Stand here," he said.

She did.

"Now look at that rock formation," he said.

She followed his gaze.

The narrow formation they had noticed earlier stood in the distance.

Still wrong.

Still not where it should be.

"What about it?" she asked.

Bill shifted one step to the left.

"Now look again."

She did.

And felt it immediately.

The angle had changed.

Not physically—

But relationally.

The formation seemed… closer.

No.

Not closer.

Better aligned.

Alex's breath caught slightly.

"That's not—" she started.

Then stopped.

Because it was.

"Do you see it?" Bill asked.

"Yes," she said quietly.

Mercer stepped closer. "What am I missing?"

Alex didn't look away from the formation.

"Move here," she said, gesturing to Bill's previous position.

Mercer did.

He looked out.

Then frowned.

"I don't—"

"Step left," Alex said.

He did.

Then—

He stopped.

"I see it," he said.

Behind them, Varn watched.

His team remained still, observing.

Not interfering.

Not commenting.

But very much paying attention.

Bill moved again.

This time faster.

Still controlled.

But with purpose.

Alex followed.

Mercer followed.

They shifted positions relative to landmarks.

Testing.

Comparing.

Adjusting.

"It's not random," Alex said.

Bill nodded.

"No."

Mercer frowned. "Then what is it?"

Bill stopped.

Looked at the terrain.

Then said—

"It's bending."

Mercer stared at him. "The ground isn't bending."

Bill shook his head. "Not the ground."

Alex felt it click.

"The relationships are," she said.

Bill nodded.

They stood in silence for a moment.

Letting that settle.

Alex turned slowly, looking across the terrain again.

But this time—

She wasn't just looking at it.

She was looking *through* it.

Watching how things lined up.

Or didn't.

"Paths aren't straight," she said.

"No," Bill replied.

"They look straight," Mercer added.

"Yes."

"But they're not."

"No."

Alex walked forward several steps.

Then stopped.

Turned.

Looked back.

The beacon they had placed earlier—

Wasn't where it should be.

Not by distance.

By alignment.

She turned back to Bill.

"This is why the grid failed," she said.

"Yes."

"They weren't moving wrong."

"No."

"They were being moved."

Bill shook his head.

"Not moved," he said.

"Then what?"

He looked at her.

"Shifted," he said.

Mercer ran a hand through his hair.

"That's not a condition we can work with," he said.

Bill looked at him.

"It is," he said.

"How?"

Bill didn't answer immediately.

Then—

"By finding what doesn't shift," he said.

Alex almost smiled.

"You said that before," she said.

"Yes."

"And it still sounds impossible."

"Yes."

Bill turned again.

Scanning.

Not for movement.

Not for signals.

For consistency.

"There," he said.

Alex followed his gaze.

A cluster of rocks.

Unremarkable.

Low.

Stable.

"What about it?" Mercer asked.

Bill didn't answer.

He started walking.

They followed.

Carefully.

As they approached—

Alex watched closely.

The cluster behaved differently.

Not perfectly stable—

But less affected.

Less drift.

Less misalignment.

"It's holding better," she said.

Bill nodded.

He stopped just short of the cluster.

Then turned.

"Look back," he said.

Alex did.

The terrain behind them—

Still wrong.

Still shifting.

But from here—

It was easier to understand.

Easier to see how things didn't line up.

"This is a reference point," Bill said.

Mercer frowned. "It's just a rock formation."

Bill shook his head. "It's consistent."

Alex looked at it again.

Not at what it was—

But at how it behaved.

And he was right.

It held.

Not perfectly.

But enough.

"Then we build from here," she said.

Bill nodded.

Behind them, Varn finally stepped forward.

"You've found one," he said.

Bill looked at him.

"Yes."

Varn studied the cluster.

Then the terrain beyond it.

Then back again.

"We identified similar points," he said. "But we couldn't use them."

Bill's expression didn't change.

"You tried to map them," he said.

"Yes."

"That won't work."

Varn watched him.

"No," he said quietly. "It didn't."

Alex looked between them.

"You knew this was happening," she said.

Varn met her gaze.

"We knew something was happening," he said.

"That's not the same thing."

"No."

Bill turned away from them both.

Back toward the open terrain.

Back toward the shifting relationships.

Back toward the problem.

"We can reach them," he said.

Alex looked at him.

"You're sure?"

Bill nodded once.

"Yes."

Mercer exhaled slowly.

"How many are still out there?" he asked.

Jonas, standing nearby, answered.

"Seven," he said.

The number settled heavily.

Seven people.

Somewhere in a world that didn't hold still.

Alex looked at the terrain again.

Then back at Bill.

"We're not chasing signals," she said.

"No," he replied.

"We're not using the grid."

"No."

"Then what are we doing?" Mercer asked.

Bill looked at the shifting world of Asterra-9.

At the subtle distortions.

At the patterns that didn't exist—

Until you knew how to see them.

"We're following the structure underneath it," he said.

No one spoke.

Because now—

For the first time—

They weren't just reacting to the problem.

They were beginning to understand it.

And understanding it—

Meant they might survive it.

The wind moved again across the open land.

Unchanged.

Unaware.

But the people standing on it—

Were starting to see something deeper.

Something hidden.

Something that had already taken seven lives out of reach—

And wasn't finished yet.

Chapter 8 — The Missing Don't Stay Still

They didn't leave the rock cluster immediately. Not because they were unsure, but because, for the first time since landing, they had something that held. Not perfectly, not absolutely, but enough.

Alex stood near the edge of the formation, watching the terrain beyond it. From here, the world still looked open, still calm, still unchanged. But now she could see it—the subtle misalignment, the way distances didn't quite resolve, the way positions felt negotiable.

She exhaled slowly. "I don't like this," she said.

Bill stood a few steps away, looking outward. "No," he said.

"That wasn't reassurance."

"It wasn't meant to be."

She almost smiled.

Mercer moved closer, checking his unit again. "Signal is back," he said.

Alex turned. "Same one?"

"No. Different signature."

That tightened something in her chest. "Another survivor."

"Yes."

"Lock it."

"I'm trying," Mercer replied. "But it won't hold."

Bill stepped closer. "Show me."

Mercer adjusted the display, projecting a shifting indicator into the air. The signal marker flickered, jumped, and adjusted, never settling in one place for more than a second.

Alex frowned. "That's worse than before."

"Yes," Mercer said.

"Or more accurate," Bill added.

They both looked at him. "What do you mean?" Alex asked.

Bill studied the shifting marker. "It's not moving randomly."

"It looks random," Mercer replied.

Bill shook his head. "It's moving relative to us."

Alex felt that settle into place. "Not a fixed point."

"No."

"Then what is it?"

Bill didn't answer immediately. He was watching the marker, then the terrain, then both. "Call out," he said.

Mercer hesitated. "What?"

"Try to reach them."

Mercer activated his comm. "This is Survey Authority. If you can hear me, respond."

For a moment, nothing. Then a broken response came through. "…hear—" Static followed. "…can't—hold—" The signal fractured, returned briefly—"…where are you—"—and cut again.

Alex stepped closer. "That's close," she said.

"Yes," Mercer replied. "But I can't fix the position."

Bill nodded once. "Then don't."

Alex gave him a look. "That's becoming your solution to everything."

"It's working."

She exhaled. "Then what do we do?"

Bill turned slightly. "Find where they intersect us."

Mercer frowned. "That's not how location works."

"No," Bill said. "It isn't."

Alex looked out across the terrain again, then back at the shifting marker, then at Bill. "Walk it," she said.

He nodded and started moving.

This time they didn't follow a line—they followed a relationship. Bill moved slowly, not toward the signal but through the space around it, adjusting, pausing, and reorienting. Alex stayed close, matching his position and watching what he watched—not the marker, but the terrain, the way things lined up or didn't.

Mercer followed, less certain but learning. Behind them, Varn's team spread wider, observing from different angles—not interfering, but tracking.

"There," Bill said.

Alex looked. At first she saw nothing. Then movement—faint, then again.

"I see them," she said.

Mercer turned. "Where?"

Alex pointed. "Two hundred meters—slightly right of that ridge."

Mercer looked, then stopped. "I have nothing there."

Bill didn't look at the unit. He was already moving. "Stay aligned."

Alex followed carefully. As they moved, the figures ahead became clearer—not one, but two.

"Two survivors," Alex said.

Mercer checked his unit again. "Signal confirms two, but position—"

"Doesn't matter," Alex said.

The figures ahead were moving, but not together. One walked steadily while the other stopped, turned, and walked again, as if trying to follow something that wouldn't stay still.

"Call them," Alex said.

Mercer activated comm. "This is Survey Authority. Hold your position."

One of the figures stopped, turned, and looked—not at them, but past them.

"They don't see us," Mercer said.

"No," Bill replied. "They're misaligned."

Alex stepped forward. "Hey!"

The closer figure reacted, but not correctly, turning toward a point several meters off.

"They're drifting," Alex said.

Bill nodded.

The second figure stopped completely, then turned slowly, as if trying to find something.

"Stay where you are!" Mercer called.

The first figure took another step, then another.

"Stop," Bill said.

Everyone froze.

The first figure kept moving, not toward them, but toward somewhere else.

"They're crossing out of alignment," Alex said.

"Yes," Bill replied.

He moved fast but controlled. Alex followed immediately.

"Stay with him!" Mercer called.

The distance between them and the survivors didn't behave correctly. It stretched, compressed, and shifted. Alex felt it now—not just visually, but physically—the sense that space itself wasn't holding still.

"Left," Bill said.

She adjusted.

"Now forward."

She moved.

The first survivor was closer, then farther, then closer again. Alex reached out too soon.

"Not yet," Bill said.

He adjusted again—one step, two, then a pause. The second survivor flickered, not visually but relationally, like their position was slipping.

"They're going," Alex said.

Bill didn't answer.

He moved again. This time, exactly.

"Now."

Alex stepped forward, hand out. Contact.

For a moment, the same resistance—the subtle stutter. Then it resolved. The survivor stumbled forward into alignment, into place. Alex grabbed their arm, steadying them.

"You're okay."

The second survivor was still drifting. Bill was already moving. He reached them, adjusted, aligned, and pulled them back.

Two more. Recovered.

They stood together now, breathing, disoriented but present.

"How—" one of them said. "We were right there—"

Alex shook her head. "No. You weren't."

Mercer moved in quickly. "Vitals stable."

Bill stepped back slightly, watching and confirming. Behind them, Varn approached slowly, his expression changed—less controlled, more certain.

"They're not staying in one place," he said.

Alex looked at him. "No." She turned back to the terrain. "The missing don't stay still."

No one argued, because now they understood something new—something worse.

It wasn't just that people were lost. Even if you knew where they were, they wouldn't stay there.

Bill looked out across the shifting terrain. "We have to move faster."

Alex nodded, because now they weren't just searching.

They were racing against a world that refused to hold still.

Chapter 9 — Where the Map Breaks

They brought the two survivors back to the rock cluster, not because it was safe, but because it was less unstable. On Asterra-9, that distinction mattered.

The survivors—both exhausted and visibly shaken—sat near the base of the formation while Mercer completed a quick assessment. "Vitals are stable," he said. "Disorientation, mild dehydration, elevated stress levels—but nothing critical."

Alex crouched nearby, watching them closely. "Can you focus?" she asked gently.

One of them—a woman in her early thirties—nodded slowly. "I think so. It's… clearer now."

"What do you remember?"

The woman hesitated before answering. "We were following the grid. Standard sweep pattern. Everything was normal."

Alex exchanged a glance with Bill. Same as Jonas.

"What changed?"

The woman swallowed. "We couldn't match anything anymore. Markers didn't line up. Distances felt wrong. We thought it was calibration—so we recalibrated."

"That didn't help."

"No," the woman said quietly. "It made it worse."

Bill stood a short distance away, watching the terrain. He hadn't spoken since the rescue. Alex recognized that. It meant he was working.

Mercer stepped closer to him. "We need to establish a search grid," he said.

Bill didn't look at him. "No."

Mercer frowned. "We need structure."

Bill nodded once. "Yes."

"Then we map it."

"No."

Mercer exhaled sharply. "You're not giving me a lot to work with."

Bill turned slightly. "The map is wrong," he said.

Mercer gestured toward his unit. "It's all we have."

Bill shook his head. "It's what we had."

Alex stood and moved toward them. "He's right," she said.

Mercer looked at her. "We can't operate without coordinates."

"We already aren't."

Mercer opened his mouth, then stopped, because he knew it was true.

Alex stepped closer to the projected display on his unit. The grid hovered in the air—clean, precise, reliable.

Except it wasn't.

"Show me the last known positions."

Mercer adjusted the display. Markers appeared—Jonas, the two survivors they had just recovered, and several others still unaccounted for.

Alex studied the layout, then looked up, then back again. "It's broken."

Mercer crossed his arms. "That's not helpful."

Alex shook her head. "No. It's important." She pointed to the grid. "This assumes fixed relationships between positions."

"Yes."

"That assumption is wrong."

Bill watched her, not surprised, just confirming.

Alex turned back to the display. "These points aren't fixed. They're drifting relative to each other."

Mercer frowned. "That's not how coordinate systems work."

"No," Alex said. "It's not."

She deactivated the projection. The clean grid disappeared, leaving only the open terrain.

"That's the problem."

Mercer looked at her, then at Bill, then back at the terrain. "If we can't map it," he said slowly, "then we can't navigate it."

Bill shook his head. "We can."

"How?"

Bill stepped toward the edge of the rock cluster, toward the shifting world beyond it. "By not pretending it's something it isn't."

Alex almost smiled. That was Bill—simple, direct, completely unhelpful until it wasn't.

"Then what is it?" Mercer asked.

Bill looked out across the terrain, at the subtle distortions, at the misaligned relationships, at the invisible structure beneath it all. "It's a system."

Alex felt that settle. "Yes."

"A system of what?" Mercer asked.

Bill didn't answer immediately. "Movement."

Alex stepped closer. "Not objects moving."

Bill nodded. "Relationships moving."

Mercer shook his head. "That's not something we can track."

Bill looked at him. "We don't track it. We follow it."

Mercer exhaled. "That's not a plan."

Alex folded her arms. "It's the only one that's working."

Mercer looked at the survivors, at Jonas, at the terrain, at the broken map, then nodded once. "Then we do it your way."

Bill didn't respond. He was already moving.

Alex followed.

This time, they didn't bring the unit as a guide—only as a reference.

Bill stepped off the stable ground of the rock cluster and into the drift. The shift was immediate, subtle but unmistakable.

Alex felt it again—that slight disorientation, that sense that position was no longer absolute.

"Stay close," Bill said.

She did.

Behind them, Mercer and the others followed carefully. The survivors remained at the cluster under watch from Varn's team.

"We'll establish a return anchor here," Mercer said.

Bill nodded once, then continued forward.

The terrain ahead stretched open—unchanged, untroubled, impossible.

Bill moved slowly, never in a straight line.

Alex watched his steps, trying to understand the pattern, but there wasn't one—not a visible one.

"How do you know where to go?" she asked.

Bill didn't look at her. "I don't."

That didn't help.

She exhaled. "Then what are you doing?"

He paused. "I'm finding where not to go."

Alex blinked, then it clicked.

"You're eliminating misalignment."

Bill nodded.

She looked at the terrain again, this time differently—not looking for a path, but looking for stability.

"Left," she said.

Bill adjusted.

"Too far."

He corrected.

They moved together now, not following a map, not following a signal, but following alignment.

After several minutes, Bill stopped. "There."

Alex looked. At first, nothing. Then a flicker. Movement.

Another survivor.

Mercer's unit beeped. "Signal confirms."

Alex allowed herself a small smile. "We're getting better at this."

Bill didn't respond. He stepped forward.

The map was gone. The grid was gone. Everything they had relied on—gone.

And yet they were finding people.

Alex looked back once toward the rock cluster, toward the one place that still held, then forward again.

"This is how we do it."

Bill nodded.

Because now they understood something fundamental.

The map hadn't failed.

It had never applied.

And once they let it go, they could finally see where the world actually was.

Chapter 10 — The Ones Between

The next survivor did not come back easily. That was the first thing Alex understood—not because Bill was uncertain, not because the path failed, and not because they had lost the method they were beginning to form, but because what they were trying to recover this time was not simply displaced. It was partially gone.

The figure stood ahead of them near a low rise of stone and hard-packed soil. At first glance, the person seemed perfectly ordinary—upright, human, still enough to be mistaken for someone who had simply stopped to wait. But the longer Alex looked, the less stable that impression became.

She narrowed her eyes. "What is that?" she asked quietly.

Mercer checked his unit. "Signal is weak, but present."

"That's not what I meant."

Bill had already stopped. He didn't answer right away.

Alex took one step to the side for a better angle. The figure ahead seemed to shift—not in position, not by movement, but by certainty. For one instant the survivor looked fully present, solid and real. The next, something about the outline felt slightly off, as though the world had failed to finish drawing the edges correctly.

Alex felt a chill move down her arms. "They're not fully here," she said.

Bill nodded once. "No."

Mercer stared out at the figure, his expression tightening. "How is that possible?"

No one answered, because no one knew.

The survivor moved—or seemed to. A slight turn of the head, a shift in posture, a hand lifting halfway and then stopping. But the motion didn't resolve cleanly. It lagged, not by time, but by placement. Alex had the unsettling impression of watching someone occupy two neighboring possibilities at once.

"That's worse," she said.

Bill didn't argue. "Yes."

The wind passed lightly over the open ground, carrying dust in a faint ribbon past their boots. Ahead, the figure turned again. This time the face came partly into view. Alex couldn't make out details yet, but she could tell it was one of the survey team—alive, standing, and somehow not entirely reachable.

Mercer swallowed. "Can they even hear us?"

Bill studied the space between them. "Maybe."

"Maybe," Mercer repeated. "That's becoming a difficult word out here."

Alex didn't look away from the figure. "Call anyway."

Mercer raised his comm. "Survey team member ahead—if you can hear me, stay where you are. Do not move."

For a moment, nothing happened. Then the figure reacted with a slight turn, a pause, and a shift in the shoulders.

"They heard that," Alex said.

"Or something close to it," Bill replied.

He started forward carefully. Alex moved with him, and Mercer followed. This time even Varn came closer than before, though he remained several paces behind, watching with focused attention.

The terrain between them and the survivor looked no different from any they had already crossed—open, walkable, quiet—but the feel of it changed with each step. Alex noticed it first as pressure behind her eyes, a subtle strain as though her perception had to work harder just to confirm what should have been obvious. Then her balance shifted, not enough to stumble, just enough to remind her that every step now depended on something less reliable than solid ground.

Bill slowed. "From here on, you do exactly what I do."

Alex nodded immediately. Mercer hesitated, then nodded as well.

The survivor wavered again. This time Alex saw it clearly. One moment the woman stood near the rise; the next, she seemed offset, half a body width out of place, as if her position had slipped sideways without moving.

Alex held her breath. "They're slipping," she said.

Bill's voice remained calm. "Yes."

"How do we stop that?"

"We don't. We reach them before it worsens."

It wasn't the answer Alex wanted, but it was the right one.

They advanced. Bill angled left, then right, then stopped entirely. Alex mirrored him, and Mercer followed less smoothly but close enough.

Ahead, the survivor lifted one arm as if trying to signal. The motion came wrong—not blurred, not doubled, just slightly out of sync with itself. It was enough to tighten Alex's stomach.

"We need a fixed visual," Bill said.

Alex scanned quickly. "That rise. And the split rock behind it."

Bill nodded. "Use both."

Mercer glanced at his unit. "I'm losing the signal."

"Forget the signal," Alex said.

He didn't like it, but he obeyed.

They moved again, step by step, adjusting and pausing. Bill checked behind them occasionally, not long, just enough to confirm alignment with the last stable reference. The rock cluster was almost out of range now, but the principle held.

Ahead, the woman turned more fully toward them—or almost. Her face resolved for a moment, dust-streaked, pale, confused, and then slipped again.

Alex felt the urge to rush. Bill caught it immediately. "Don't."

"I know," she said, but she had needed the reminder.

At twenty meters, the woman spoke. The sound reached them strangely—not distorted, not distant, just displaced.

"Please—"

Thin, strained, and then her outline shifted again.

Mercer stopped. "That's bad."

Bill didn't answer. He was studying the space between them, not her, but the line.

Alex saw it then. He wasn't navigating terrain anymore. He was navigating alignment under distortion.

"Stand where I stand," Bill said.

He shifted one step right. Alex matched him, and Mercer followed. The woman became clearer—not stable, but closer.

Another step. Another adjustment. Better, then worse, then better again.

Alex felt it click. They weren't moving toward her. They were finding the angle where their positions could overlap. This wasn't distance. This was alignment.

The woman swayed. Alex's pulse jumped. "She's losing it."

Bill moved faster, still controlled. "Stay on me."

They did.

The angle changed. The woman sharpened. For one brief moment, she was fully there.

Then she slipped again.

"No," Alex whispered.

Bill stopped hard, checked left, then right, then the rise and the split rock. Then he took one diagonal step that made no visible sense.

"Now."

Alex felt it immediately. The world clicked—not fully, not comfortably, but enough.

The woman was there—solid, frightened, real.

Bill closed the distance in four strides. This time she saw him—truly saw him. Her eyes widened.

"Don't move," he said.

She froze.

He reached out. For a fraction of a second his arm met resistance—not visible, but unmistakable. Then contact.

His hand closed around her wrist. The same stutter as before, but stronger. She gasped.

Bill braced. For a moment it felt as though the world itself resisted. Then it gave.

She staggered forward. Bill caught her. Alex moved in immediately, taking her other arm.

"You're back. Stay with us."

The woman blinked, disoriented. "I—I was here—I kept trying to—" Her voice broke.

Bill steadied her. "You were between positions."

She stared at him, not understanding.

Alex didn't fully understand either, but she understood enough to know how close this had been.

Mercer scanned quickly. "Vitals elevated. Severe dehydration. Stress response high." He paused. "But she's here."

That mattered more than anything else.

Behind them, Varn approached slowly. For the first time, something in his composure shifted—not fear, not panic, but something closer to respect.

"You brought her through a partial separation," he said.

Bill glanced at him. "Is that what you call it?"

Varn paused. "We've used several terms."

"None of them explain it," Alex said.

"No," Varn admitted. "Not yet."

Leena, still recovering, looked back toward where she had been standing. "I was there," she whispered.

Bill shook his head gently. "Partly."

The word hit harder than anything else.

"What's your name?" Alex asked.

"Leena," she said. "Survey geologist."

"Can you walk?"

"I think so."

"We're taking you back to the anchor point."

Leena frowned weakly. "Anchor point?"

"It'll make sense later."

Alex didn't like that answer, but it was all they had.

They began the return carefully. Bill led. Alex stayed close beside Leena. Mercer covered the rear. Varn's team followed at a distance.

Alex looked back once. The place where Leena had stood looked ordinary, empty, as if nothing had happened.

That was what made Asterra-9 dangerous—not that it showed its threat, but that it hid it.

When they reached the rock cluster, Jonas rose immediately. The others looked up with recognition, relief, and disbelief.

Leena sank to the ground. Jonas knelt beside her. “We thought you were gone.”

She shook her head weakly. “I thought I was right in front of you.”

No one had an answer for that.

Alex stepped aside with Bill. “That was different,” she said.

“Yes.”

“Worse.”

“Yes.”

She looked out at the terrain again. “How many more like that?”

Bill didn’t answer immediately. Then he said, “All of them.”

Alex let out a slow breath. That was the only safe answer.

Behind them, Varn spoke. “The next recoveries will be harder.”

Alex didn’t turn right away. “That’s not helpful.”

“It’s preparation.”

She looked at him, then away, because he was right.

The easy rescues were over. Ahead were the ones deeper in the drift, the ones slipping beyond reach.

The ones between.

Alex looked back at Bill. He was already watching the terrain, already working ahead, with no hesitation and no pause.

Just steady forward movement.

Alex felt something settle. This wouldn’t be quick. This wouldn’t be simple. And whatever came next would demand more from all of them.

“We can still get them,” she said.

Bill looked at the horizon. “Yes.”

Not easy. Not certain. Not safe.

Just yes.

And on Asterra-9, that was enough to keep moving.

The wind moved across the open ground, calm and wide and deceptively gentle. The world looked unchanged.

But Alex knew better.

There were still people out there—not lost, not waiting, not fixed.

Slipping.

And the only way to bring them back was to reach them before "here" and "there" stopped meaning anything at all.

Chapter 11 — AEGIS Line Drawn

They didn't leave immediately. Even after Leena had been stabilized, even after the others had confirmed her condition, and even after the method—however fragile—had proven itself again, something had shifted. Not in the terrain, but in the people.

The rock cluster no longer felt like a temporary waypoint. It felt like a boundary. On one side was relative stability, recoverable ground, and a place where people could exist without slipping. On the other was the drift—the distortion, the part of Asterra-9 that didn't hold still long enough to be trusted.

Alex stood near the edge of that boundary, looking outward. She could see it more clearly now, not visually, but structurally. The terrain ahead didn't align the same way. Distances didn't resolve cleanly, and reference points didn't hold together as they should. It was like looking at a world that had been deliberately misarranged—not broken, but repositioned.

Behind her, Mercer finished another scan and lowered the unit. "They'll hold here," he said. "For now."

Alex nodded. "For now," she repeated, and the phrase carried more weight than she liked.

Varn stepped forward, not quickly and not aggressively, but with clear intent. His team shifted subtly behind him, taking positions closer to the cluster without crowding it. Alex noticed immediately.

"We need to establish limits," Varn said. His voice carried easily across the space—not raised, but firm.

Mercer turned. "Limits?"

"Yes."

Varn's gaze passed briefly over the survivors, then returned to Bill. "The deeper regions are becoming more unstable. You've seen that. Each recovery increases exposure. Each movement deeper into the drift carries higher risk."

"That's already true," Alex said.

"Yes," Varn replied. "Which is why we adjust."

Bill spoke. "No."

The word wasn't sharp or confrontational. It was simply final.

Varn looked at him. "You haven't heard the recommendation."

"I don't need to."

A brief silence followed, not tense, but precise.

Mercer shifted. "What recommendation?"

Varn answered without hesitation. "We establish a containment perimeter. This cluster becomes the operational limit. No further advance until we understand the phenomenon at a deeper level."

Alex turned fully toward him. "You're suggesting we stop."

"I'm suggesting we control the situation."

She shook her head. "That's not the same thing."

"No," he said. "It isn't."

Bill hadn't moved, but Alex could feel the shift in him. Not anger, not frustration—something quieter, more resolved.

"There are still people out there," he said.

Varn nodded. "Yes."

"And your plan is to wait."

"My plan is to prevent further loss."

Alex stepped forward. "You're not preventing loss. You're accepting it."

Varn met her gaze. "No. I'm limiting it."

That landed harder than she expected, because it wasn't careless or dismissive. It was calculated.

Mercer ran a hand along the back of his neck. "This isn't a containment scenario. It's a rescue operation."

Varn looked at him. "It was."

The words hung in the air.

Alex felt something tighten in her chest. "That's not acceptable."

Varn's expression didn't change. "Acceptability doesn't alter conditions."

Bill moved one step forward. It was enough.

"No," he said again.

Varn's attention returned fully to him.

"We continue," Bill said.

Varn studied him longer this time. "You're basing that on incomplete understanding."

Bill nodded. "Yes."

"And you still proceed."

"Yes."

Varn exhaled slowly, not in frustration, but in recognition. "You're anchoring movement through relational stability," he said. It wasn't a question.

Bill didn't answer.

"You're not using the grid," Varn continued.

"No."

"You're not following signals."

"No."

"You're… aligning."

Bill said nothing.

Alex watched closely. Varn wasn't arguing. He was confirming.

"You can reach them," Varn said quietly.

Bill met his gaze. "Yes."

Another silence followed.

Mercer spoke. "I'd like to point out that whatever we're doing—it's working."

Varn didn't look at him. "At a cost," he said.

Bill nodded. "Yes."

Alex stepped closer. "We already knew that."

Varn turned slightly toward her. "Not like this."

She frowned. "What does that mean?"

Varn hesitated only briefly. "The deeper regions are not just more unstable. They're less recoverable."

Alex felt that settle coldly.

"Meaning what?" Mercer asked.

Varn looked at him. "Meaning there is a point beyond which retrieval may not be possible."

No one spoke.

The wind moved lightly across the cluster, shifting dust in a faint line across the ground.

Alex looked out toward the drift. "How far?"

Varn didn't answer immediately. "We don't know."

That was worse.

Bill turned back toward the terrain. "We find them before that point," he said.

It wasn't a plan or a suggestion. It was a statement.

Mercer let out a breath. "That's the only approach we've got."

Varn looked at both of them, then at the survivors, then back at the world beyond the cluster. "We will not interfere," he said.

Alex blinked. "That's not what I expected you to say."

"No," Varn replied. "It isn't."

He gestured slightly to his team. "They will maintain observation. They will assist with stabilization here."

"And beyond that?" Mercer asked.

Varn looked at Bill. "Beyond that—this is your operation."

Alex felt the shift clearly. Varn wasn't withdrawing. He was yielding—not out of agreement, but out of recognition.

Bill nodded once. "That's fine."

There was no triumph in it, no satisfaction—just continuation.

Alex looked between them, then out toward the drift again. The boundary felt sharper now, more real. On one side was a place where people could still be held. On the other was a place where they might not be.

She drew in a slow breath. "We don't have time to wait."

Bill nodded. "No."

Mercer checked his unit. "Signals are still out there. Multiple."

Alex looked at Bill. "How many left?"

He didn't look at the unit. He didn't need to.

"Five."

The number settled heavier than before. Five people, somewhere in a world that didn't stay where it should.

Alex shifted slightly closer to Bill, closer to the edge.

"Then we go," she said.

Bill stepped forward.

And once again, they crossed the line.

Behind them, the rock cluster held—stable, reliable, temporary. Ahead, the drift waited, and somewhere inside it, five people were still trying to exist in a place that no longer held them properly.

Bill didn't hesitate, because out there, hesitation was something the world would not forgive.

Chapter 12 — The Center of Drift

They felt the difference almost immediately. The moment they crossed beyond the rock cluster's influence, the world lost what little consistency it had offered before. Alex felt it first in her footing. The ground was still solid, still firm, still exactly what it appeared to be, but her sense of where she stood relative to everything else began to loosen, like a point on a map that no longer agreed with its surroundings.

"Stay tight," Bill said. His voice was calm, but more compressed now, more focused.

Alex adjusted without thinking, moving closer and matching his stride and angle. Mercer followed more carefully, less confident now and more aware of the instability around them. Behind them, Varn's team remained at the cluster, watching but not following. They were on their own now.

The terrain ahead stretched wide, unchanged to the eye but fundamentally different in behavior. Bill slowed, angled slightly right, and stopped. Alex mirrored him.

"What is it?" she asked.

Bill didn't answer immediately. He was watching the horizon, then the ground, then the relationship between the two.

"It's stronger here," he said.

Alex nodded. "Yes." She didn't need instruments anymore. She could feel it.

Mercer checked anyway. “Signal scatter is increasing. I can’t isolate anything.”

Bill glanced at the unit, then back to the terrain. “Put it away.”

Mercer hesitated, then complied. It wasn’t helping.

They moved again, slower now and more deliberate. Each step required attention. Each shift required confirmation. Alex found herself relying less on sight and more on consistency—the way the ground met her feet, the way Bill moved, the way certain landmarks held together slightly better than others.

It wasn’t enough to see where they were. They had to feel when it was wrong.

“Left,” Bill said.

She adjusted.

“Now forward.”

She moved, and Mercer followed.

The pattern was forming again—not a map, not a path, but a structure.

After several minutes, Bill stopped. “There.”

Alex looked ahead. At first she saw nothing. Then something changed. Not visually, but relationally. The horizon didn’t line up. It tilted—not physically, but in the way the terrain connected to itself.

“That’s it,” she said.

Bill nodded.

Mercer squinted, then stopped mid-sentence. “I see it.”

Ahead of them, the world didn’t hold. It bent—not like a surface or a curve, but like a relationship under strain.

Alex felt her breath catch. “This is the center.”

Bill didn’t answer, but he didn’t disagree.

Mercer swallowed. “Signal density is highest here, but I still can’t isolate positions.”

"You won't," Bill said.

Alex took a slow step forward. The shift hit harder this time. The world didn't resist her movement. It reinterpreted it. She stopped immediately.

"Okay… that's worse."

Bill nodded. "Yes."

They stood at the edge of it—the place where the drift was no longer something they moved through, but something that defined the space itself.

"How many?" Alex asked quietly.

Mercer checked and shook his head. "I can't tell."

Bill looked out across the distortion. "Five."

Alex felt that settle. Five people, somewhere in this.

Not lost.

Misplaced.

She looked ahead, trying to see them, trying to find movement, trying to find anything. Then she saw it—a flicker, then another.

"Multiple," she said.

Bill nodded. "They're here."

Alex stepped slightly left. The flicker sharpened. Three figures, then two, then one.

She froze. "They're overlapping."

Bill didn't respond. He was already moving.

"Stay on me."

Alex followed. Mercer followed.

Movement now was difficult—not physically, but perceptually. Each step required correction. Each correction required trust.

The figures ahead didn't hold. They shifted, merged, and separated like positions that couldn't decide where they belonged.

"This is bad," Mercer said.

"Yes," Alex replied.

Bill didn't speak. He moved, adjusting constantly—not toward a figure, but toward alignment.

Alex matched him—step, pause, adjust.

The world resisted clarity, but not completely.

"Here," Bill said.

Alex stopped. The figures stabilized—not fully, but enough.

Five. All of them. Standing, moving, trying.

"Don't move!" Alex called.

They reacted, but not correctly—turning, shifting.

One stepped forward and vanished—not gone, but out of alignment.

"No," Mercer said.

Bill moved faster now.

This was it.

No more testing. No more gradual understanding.

This was the point Varn had warned about—the edge beyond recovery.

And they were standing on it.

"Stay with me!" Bill said.

Alex didn't hesitate. She moved.

The world broke around them—not visibly, but relationally. Positions collapsed. Distances failed.

The figures slipped.

"Now!" Bill said.

Alex stepped exactly where he stepped.

The world clicked—not stable, but aligned.

For a moment.

Bill reached the first survivor, grabbed them, and pulled them forward. Alex caught the second. Mercer the third.

Two more were still slipping.

Bill turned, moved, and adjusted again. The last two were fading.

"Hold!" he said.

Alex braced.

The world resisted harder than before, like pulling something back from a place it had already begun to leave.

Then it gave.

All five were back—present, real.

They collapsed around Bill and Alex, breathing, shaking, alive.

No one spoke, because for a moment no one trusted the world to hold the result.

Bill didn't move yet. He stood, anchoring, holding the alignment until it settled just enough.

Alex exhaled slowly. "They're here."

Bill nodded. "Yes."

Behind them, the drift continued—unchanged, unconcerned.

But they had reached into it and taken something back.

Alex looked at the survivors, then at Bill, then at the unstable world beyond.

"This isn't just a phenomenon," she said quietly.

Bill didn't answer, because he was already thinking ahead.

And Alex knew this wasn't the end of it.

Not even close.

Chapter 13 — Into the Drift

They did not celebrate. Not when all five survivors were accounted for, not when the last of them steadied on their feet, and not even when Mercer confirmed, one by one, that every vital sign had returned to normal. Relief was there, but it was quiet and contained, because no one believed they were finished.

"Move," Bill said. His tone wasn't sharp or urgent, but it carried weight.

Alex understood immediately. "This isn't stable."

"No."

The survivors were already shifting uneasily—not physically, but relationally. Alex could see it in the way they looked around, trying to confirm where they were, trying to anchor themselves to something that would hold. But nothing held for long.

"We need to get them back to the cluster," Mercer said.

"Yes," Alex replied. "Now."

Bill nodded once, then turned. "Stay on me."

This time, there was no hesitation. The group formed quickly, Bill at the front, Alex just behind and slightly to his right, the survivors between them—close enough to guide, far enough not to interfere—and Mercer at the rear, watching for drift. They moved as a single unit.

The difference was immediate. Where before Bill had moved freely, adjusting and testing as he learned, now every step carried consequence.

"Left," he said.

The group shifted.

"Hold."

They froze.

One of the survivors, a younger man, pale and wide-eyed, stumbled. Alex caught his arm before he could step out of alignment. "Stay with me."

He nodded too quickly, but he stayed.

They moved again.

The world resisted—not physically, but structurally. Alex felt it in her chest now, a subtle pressure, as though the space around them didn't want to resolve cleanly.

"How far?" Mercer asked.

Bill didn't answer, because distance didn't mean anything here.

"Just stay aligned," Alex said.

Mercer nodded.

They continued forward. The terrain shifted—not visibly, but in the way it connected. A ridge that should have been behind them lingered at the edge of vision. A landmark ahead seemed closer, then farther, then neither.

"Don't look too long at anything," Bill said.

Alex frowned. "Why?"

"Because it won't stay where you think it is."

That made sense, and didn't. She forced herself to focus on Bill instead—on his position, on his movement. That held, for now.

Behind them, one of the survivors gasped.

Alex turned slightly. "Stay with us."

"I'm trying," the man said.

Bill stopped suddenly.

The group froze.

"What is it?" Alex asked.

Bill didn't answer immediately. He looked ahead, then down, then slightly left.

"The alignment changed."

Alex felt it then—the subtle shift. The world no longer matched the path they had been following.

"We're off," Mercer said.

"Yes," Bill replied.

"How?"

Bill didn't answer.

He moved—one step, then paused, then adjusted, then another step.

Alex followed carefully. The group mirrored them.

The pressure eased slightly.

"That's it," Alex said.

Bill nodded.

They moved again, but slower now. Each step was tested. Each shift confirmed.

The survivors stayed closer than before. They had learned—or maybe they were just afraid. Either worked.

After several minutes, Alex saw it—the rock cluster, faint and distant, but there.

"Visual," she said.

Mercer exhaled. "Thank God."

Bill didn't respond, because the hardest part wasn't getting there.

It was getting there without losing anyone.

"Stay tight," he said.

They moved.

The cluster grew clearer. The ground felt more stable. The pressure eased—not completely, but enough.

Then one of the survivors slipped.

It wasn't a fall. It was a shift—sideways, out of alignment.

"No!" Mercer said.

Alex turned sharply. The man was there, then not, then there again—but wrong.

Misaligned.

Bill moved instantly. "Hold position!"

Everyone froze.

Bill stepped toward the man, carefully and precisely. The world resisted again, but not as strongly—not yet.

Bill adjusted—one step, then two.

Then contact.

He grabbed the man's arm. The same stutter, the same resistance, and then it resolved.

The man staggered back into place.

Alex exhaled. "Stay with us."

This time, no one needed reminding.

They moved again, faster now, because they were close.

And the world seemed to know it.

The drift intensified—not wildly, but enough. As though the closer they came to stability, the harder it became to reach it.

"Now," Bill said.

They crossed the final distance and stepped back into alignment.

The rock cluster held. The pressure dropped. The world settled—not perfectly, but enough.

They were back.

All of them.

No one moved for several seconds. No one spoke, because the difference was overwhelming.

The survivors collapsed where they stood. Mercer began scanning immediately.

Alex stood beside Bill, looking back toward the drift.

"That got harder," she said.

Bill nodded. "Yes."

"And that was coming out."

"Yes."

She looked at him. "How bad is it going to be going in?"

Bill didn't answer right away.

Then he said, "Worse."

Alex nodded. That matched what she felt.

Behind them, Varn approached. "You reached the center," he said.

Bill didn't respond.

Varn looked at the survivors, then back at the drift. "And you brought them all back."

Bill nodded once. "Yes."

Varn studied him longer than before. "You shouldn't have been able to do that."

Bill met his gaze. "We did."

Varn didn't argue, because he had seen it.

And now the boundary had shifted again—not just in the terrain, but in what was possible.

Alex looked out across Asterra-9. The world still looked calm, still open, still unchanged.

But she knew now they had gone as far as they could.

And the next step would not be about rescue.

It would be about understanding.

And whatever this world was doing, it wasn't finished with them yet.

Chapter 14 — What Holds

They did not move immediately this time. The survivors had been stabilized, their vitals steady and awareness returning. For the first time since they had entered the drift, everyone was accounted for. And still, no one relaxed.

Alex stood near the edge of the rock cluster, arms folded lightly, eyes fixed on the open terrain beyond. It looked the same—calm, wide, unchanged—but now that meant nothing.

Behind her, Mercer finished another scan and lowered his unit. "They're holding," he said. "All of them."

Alex nodded. "For now."

He didn't argue.

A quiet settled over the group, not relief but something closer to recalibration. They had gone out, reached the center, and brought everyone back. In doing so, they had learned something dangerous.

Bill stood apart from the others, not far but separate. He wasn't watching the survivors or the team. He was watching the drift.

Alex studied him for a moment, then stepped over. "You're already ahead," she said.

"Yes."

"What are we missing?"

That made him pause—not long, but enough.

"Structure."

Alex frowned slightly. "We've been working with structure."

"No."

He turned slightly, looking not at the terrain but through it. "We've been reacting to it."

That landed. Alex shifted her stance. "So we stop reacting," she said.

Bill nodded once. "Yes."

"And start what?"

Bill didn't answer immediately. This wasn't about movement or alignment or rescue. This was about understanding something that had already proven it didn't behave like anything they knew.

Behind them, Varn approached again—not intruding, but present. "You've reached the limit of recovery," he said.

Alex didn't turn. "That's what you said before."

"And now you've confirmed it."

Bill finally looked at him. "No."

Varn's expression didn't change. "What have you confirmed, then?"

Bill glanced back toward the drift. "That it holds."

Silence followed.

Mercer frowned. "That's not what it looks like."

"No," Bill said. "It isn't."

Alex stepped closer. "Explain."

Bill took a slow breath. "The survivors weren't lost. They were displaced."

"We know that."

Bill shook his head. "No."

He looked at them now, all of them. "We've been treating displacement like instability."

Alex felt something shift. "But it's not."

"What is it?" Mercer asked.

Bill looked back out across the terrain. "It's consistent."

That hung in the air.

Alex shook her head slowly. "That doesn't match anything we've seen."

"Yes, it does."

He stepped toward the edge of the cluster. "Everything that moved moved according to something."

Alex followed his line of thought. "The relationships."

Bill nodded. "Not random."

Mercer folded his arms. "Then what determines it?"

Bill didn't answer immediately, because this was the part they hadn't reached yet.

"The same thing that lets us reach them," he said finally.

Alex frowned. "Alignment?"

Bill shook his head. "Closer than that."

She waited. He didn't rush it.

"Reference."

That word landed differently.

Alex looked back across the terrain, then down at the rock cluster. "Something holds everything else in place," she said slowly.

Bill nodded.

Mercer's expression shifted. "Like a baseline."

"Yes."

"A fixed point?"

Bill hesitated, then said, "No."

That stopped them.

"Then what?" Alex asked.

Bill looked at the cluster beneath their feet. "Not fixed," he said. "Stable."

The distinction mattered.

Alex felt it settle. Fixed meant permanent. Stable meant holding long enough to matter.

"That's why this works," she said, glancing at the cluster.

Bill nodded. "It holds better than everything else."

Mercer stepped forward slightly. "You're saying the entire drift is structured around relative stability?"

Bill didn't answer. He didn't need to. They had seen it, walked it, survived it.

Alex looked out again, this time differently—not searching for survivors, but searching for anchors.

"Then there are more," she said.

"Yes."

Varn spoke quietly behind them. "We've identified irregularities in the terrain. We didn't understand what they were."

Bill didn't look back. "You do now."

Varn didn't respond, because that was true.

Alex turned slightly. "If we can find those points—"

"We can map the system," Mercer finished.

Bill shook his head. "No."

Mercer exhaled. "You're going to tell me why that won't work."

"Yes."

"Because it won't stay mapped."

Alex nodded slowly. "But we can move between them."

Bill looked at her. "Yes."

That was the shift.

Not mapping.

Navigation.

Dynamic.

Alex felt something sharpen inside her. "This isn't just a phenomenon."

Bill didn't respond, because now they were finally asking the right question—not how to survive it, but what it was.

Behind them, Mercer glanced down at his unit again, then back up. "We've been trying to impose order."

Alex nodded. "But the order is already there."

Bill's expression didn't change. "Yes."

A quiet settled again, different this time—not uncertainty, but recognition.

Alex looked out across Asterra-9. The drift no longer felt like chaos. It felt like something unfamiliar—structured, intentional.

And that was worse.

Because chaos could be survived, but structure had purpose.

She exhaled slowly. "So what holds it?"

Bill didn't answer right away. For the first time since they had arrived, he hesitated.

Then, quietly, he said, "I don't know."

That was the most honest thing he had said yet, and the most dangerous.

Because now they understood something clearly.

They weren't dealing with a broken world.

They were standing inside something that worked exactly the way it was supposed to.

They just didn't understand the rules yet.

And until they did, they were still at risk of being pulled out of place, just like the others.

The wind moved across the open ground again, calm and wide and unchanged.

But now they knew better.

Whatever Asterra-9 was doing, it wasn't random.

It was consistent.

And that meant there was something underneath it—something holding it all together.

And sooner or later, they were going to find it.

Chapter 15 — The First Anchor

They didn't rush back into the drift, and that alone marked the change. Before, every step outward had been driven by urgency—the need to reach someone before they were lost. Now everyone was here, alive and stable, which meant, for the first time, they had something more dangerous than urgency. They had time to think.

Alex stood near the edge of the rock cluster, watching Bill. He hadn't moved far—just a few steps beyond the others, close enough to return in seconds and far enough to feel the shift.

"You're going back in," she said.

"Yes."

"Not for a rescue."

"No."

She let that settle. This would be different.

Behind them, Mercer approached more slowly than usual, less resistance in his posture and more caution. "If we're doing this," he said, "we do it deliberately."

Bill glanced at him. "Yes."

Mercer exhaled once. "That's new."

Bill didn't respond.

Varn remained farther back, observing—not intervening, but very much present.

"What's the plan?" Alex asked.

Bill looked out across the drift. "We find another stable point."

Mercer nodded slowly. "Another anchor."

Bill didn't correct him.

Alex followed Bill's gaze. The terrain looked no different than before—calm, open, unchanged—but now she wasn't looking for movement. She was looking for what held.

"How do we identify it?" she asked.

Bill stepped forward, then another step, then stopped. "The same way we did before."

Alex frowned slightly. "That wasn't exactly controlled."

"No," Bill said. "It wasn't." He glanced down briefly, then back up. "This time it is."

That was enough. Alex stepped forward to join him. Mercer followed after a short hesitation.

"Hold position here," Bill said to the others.

They did.

Now it was just the three of them.

Bill moved first, not fast and not cautious in the old sense, but intentional. Each step was placed. Each shift was measured.

Alex matched him, but this time she wasn't just following. She was watching for the same things—the way the horizon aligned, the way landmarks held or slipped, and the way space felt when it worked.

Mercer followed more quietly now, with less arguing and more observing.

After several minutes, Bill stopped. Alex looked ahead. At first there was nothing. Then she felt it—a subtle difference. The pressure eased, not gone but reduced.

"Here," Bill said.

Alex nodded slowly. "Yes."

Mercer looked around. "I don't see anything."

"That's the point," Alex said.

She stepped slightly to the left. The feeling sharpened. She stepped back and it eased again.

"Stand here."

Mercer moved into position, paused, then nodded. "I feel it."

Bill remained still, studying the area. "Not fixed," he said.

"Stable," Alex replied.

Mercer looked between them. "That's becoming a very important distinction."

"Yes," Bill said.

They stood for a moment, letting the space settle around them, testing it.

Alex shifted her weight slightly. The ground held more than it should have.

"This is smaller," she said.

"Yes."

The rock cluster had been broad, clear, and strong. This was not.

"How stable?" Mercer asked.

Bill stepped outward. The shift returned, stronger. He stepped back and it eased.

"Not enough to hold a group."

Alex understood. "Transit point."

Bill looked at her. "Yes."

That changed everything. It wasn't a place to stay. It was a place to pass through.

Mercer's expression sharpened. "So we move anchor to anchor."

"Yes."

Alex felt something click into place. This was navigation—not survival, not rescue, but movement through structure.

"We test it," she said.

Bill nodded.

He stepped outward again into the drift. Alex followed. Mercer hesitated, then followed as well.

The shift returned immediately, stronger than before, but now they expected it.

Bill adjusted, one step and then another. Alex matched him, not perfectly but closer. She felt the difference. She wasn't just following anymore. She was beginning to understand.

Mercer stumbled slightly, then corrected. "I almost lost it."

"But you didn't," Alex said.

Bill angled toward a distant rise, not because it was visible, but because it aligned. After several steps, he stopped.

Alex felt it again—the easing.

"Second anchor," she said.

Bill nodded.

Mercer exhaled. "That was faster."

"Yes."

Alex looked back. The first point was gone—not physically, but relationally. She couldn't place it anymore.

"That's a problem."

Bill shook his head. "No."

She looked at him.

"You don't go back," he said.

That settled it. Forward only.

Mercer frowned. "That's not how navigation works."

"No," Alex said. "It isn't."

But it was how this worked.

Bill looked ahead again. There was something different now—not in the terrain, but in their approach.

They weren't searching.

They were following structure.

"Again," Bill said.

They moved.

This time faster. More confident. Not reckless. No longer guessing.

Alex felt it clearly now. The anchors weren't random. They were distributed and connected—not visible, but real.

After several more transitions, Bill stopped again, this time longer.

Alex looked around. The space felt different—stronger, more defined.

"This one holds."

Bill stepped outward. The shift resisted harder than before. He stepped back and it stabilized.

"Yes."

Mercer looked around. "This could support a team."

Alex nodded. "A forward position."

Bill looked back toward the cluster—or where it had been—then forward again.

They were farther than before, and still they held.

Alex felt something shift inside her—not fear, not exactly, but something closer to realization.

"We can move through this," she said.

Bill nodded. "Yes."

Mercer exhaled slowly. "That changes everything."

Bill didn't respond, because he was already looking ahead—further, deeper.

Alex followed his gaze. For the first time, she didn't just see danger. She saw possibility.

And that was even more dangerous.

The wind moved across Asterra-9 again, unchanged.

But now they were no longer reacting to it. They were beginning to understand how to move within it.

And that meant the next step wouldn't be survival.

It would be exploration.

And whatever lay deeper in the structure of this world, they were going to find it.

Chapter 16 — Something That Shouldn't Be There

They didn't return immediately, and that was the first decision. The second was to keep going.

Bill stood at the forward anchor, looking out into the drift. The space ahead no longer felt like open terrain. It felt layered, as if something beneath the surface was influencing everything above it.

Alex stepped beside him. "You see it too," she said.

Bill nodded. "Yes."

"What is it?"

Bill didn't answer right away, not because he didn't have a thought, but because he wasn't ready to define it yet. "It's different," he said.

Alex folded her arms lightly, studying the space ahead. The terrain still appeared unchanged—no visible structures, no obvious formations, nothing that should draw attention—but something about it held differently. Not stronger, not weaker, but more organized.

Behind them, Mercer adjusted his stance. "This is where we stop pretending we understand what we're doing," he said.

Alex glanced back at him. "That moment was several chapters ago."

Mercer almost smiled. "Fair."

Bill moved, not far, just enough to test the boundary of the anchor they stood on. The shift responded immediately, stronger than before but not chaotic. It felt directed, as if the instability itself had gradients.

He stepped back. "It's not uniform," he said.

Alex nodded. "No. It's not."

She looked ahead again, narrowing her focus, not on landmarks, but on how the space behaved when she shifted her perspective. After a few seconds, she saw it.

"There," she said quietly.

Mercer stepped closer. "I don't—" Then he stopped.

A faint distortion appeared. Not a flicker, not a shift, but something more stable than that.

"Is that… fixed?" Mercer asked.

Bill shook his head. "No."

Alex tilted her head slightly. "It's holding," she said.

That was different. Everything they had encountered so far had required constant adjustment and correction. This did not. It remained.

Bill stepped forward. Alex followed immediately. Mercer hesitated only a moment before joining them.

The movement toward it was easier than expected. Not simple, but guided. That alone was enough to raise concern.

"This shouldn't be easier," Mercer said quietly.

"No," Alex agreed. "It shouldn't."

They slowed as they approached. The distortion resolved, and for the first time since arriving on Asterra-9, they saw something that did not belong to the terrain.

It wasn't large—perhaps three meters across, low to the ground, dark, and smooth. Not like rock, not like soil. It looked shaped.

Alex stopped. "That's not natural," she said.

"No," Bill replied.

Mercer circled slightly, keeping distance. "I'm not getting any readable signal from it," he said. "No energy output. No identifiable composition."

"That doesn't mean it's inactive," Alex said.

"No," Mercer replied. "It doesn't."

Bill stepped closer, carefully. The space around the object didn't distort the way the rest of the drift did. If anything, it stabilized.

Alex felt it immediately. The pressure eased. The alignment held.

"This is stronger than the anchors," she said.

Bill nodded. "Yes."

Mercer looked between them. "Then this is the source?"

Bill didn't answer.

He crouched slightly, studying the surface. It was perfectly smooth, with no markings and no visible seams, and yet it felt intentional.

Alex stepped closer. The moment she crossed a certain threshold, the world snapped into clarity—not completely, but more than anywhere else.

She stopped. "Bill," she said quietly.

He looked at her.

"This is stabilizing everything around it."

He nodded. "Yes."

Mercer took one cautious step closer, then another, and stopped beside them. "I don't like this," he said.

Alex didn't disagree. "Because it's working."

That was the problem. The drift had been chaotic, dangerous, unpredictable. This was controlled.

Bill reached out, not touching, just close enough to feel. The air near the surface felt steady, like standing inside a boundary that held reality together more tightly than the space outside it.

"This isn't part of the terrain," Alex said.

"No," Bill replied.

Mercer looked at the object again. "Then what is it?"

No one answered, because this was new—not just another layer of the same phenomenon, but something deeper, something that didn't just exist within the drift but defined it.

Bill stood, looking down at the object, then out at the surrounding terrain, then back again. "It's connected," he said.

Alex nodded slowly. "To everything."

Mercer exhaled. "That's not what I wanted to hear."

Bill didn't respond, because the implication was already clear. If this was one, there could be more. And if there were more, then the drift wasn't a condition. It was a system.

Alex stepped back slightly. The clarity faded just enough to notice.

"That confirms it," she said.

Bill looked at her.

"It's generating stability," she continued.

He shook his head. "No."

She frowned. "Then what?"

Bill looked back at the object. "It's enforcing it."

That word landed harder.

Alex felt it settle. This wasn't passive. This wasn't environmental. This was active.

Mercer looked at both of them. "You're saying this is controlling the drift?"

Bill didn't answer, because he didn't need to. They had seen enough.

Alex looked down at the object again—something that shouldn't be there, something that didn't belong to the world and yet held it together.

"We need to report this," Mercer said.

Bill didn't move. "Not yet," he said.

Alex glanced at him. "Why?"

Bill looked out across the terrain, because now they were no longer just observers. They were standing inside the system, and they didn't yet understand what it would do if it realized they were there.

"This changes everything," Alex said quietly.

Bill nodded. "Yes."

For the first time since they had arrived, the question was no longer how to survive Asterra-9, but who—or what—had built it.

The wind moved across the open ground again, unchanged, but now it felt like it was passing over something hidden—something watching, something waiting.

And they had just taken the first step toward finding it.

Chapter 17 — The Response

They did not touch it. That was the first decision, not spoken or debated, but simply understood.

Bill stepped back from the object, giving it space—not out of fear, but out of caution. Alex followed his movement, watching the way the clarity shifted as distance increased. The further they moved from it, the more the familiar instability returned, subtle at first and then unmistakable.

"It's localized," she said.

"Yes," Bill replied.

Mercer remained where he was for a moment longer, studying the surface. "No emissions," he said. "No heat, no signal, nothing measurable."

"That doesn't mean it's inactive," Alex said.

Mercer nodded. "I know."

He stepped back, and the shift returned immediately.

"That's not passive," he added.

No one disagreed.

They stood just outside the strongest field of stability now, close enough to feel its influence and far enough to recognize its boundary. Alex looked out across the terrain, then back at the object, then back again.

"The anchors," she said slowly. "They're not random."

Bill didn't respond, but she knew he was following.

"They're connected to this," she continued.

Mercer frowned slightly. "You're saying everything we've been using—every stable point—"

"—is part of a larger structure," Alex finished.

Bill nodded once. "Yes."

That changed the scale. This wasn't just a localized phenomenon, not just a field, not just environmental instability. This was a system, and they were standing at one of its nodes.

Mercer looked down at the object again. "How many of these are there?" he asked.

Bill didn't answer, because that question didn't have a safe answer.

Alex exhaled slowly. "If there's one here…"

"There are more," Mercer said.

Bill didn't contradict it.

The wind moved lightly across the ground, carrying a faint line of dust past the object's edge. For a moment, nothing happened.

Then Alex stiffened. "Did you see that?"

Mercer turned. "See what?"

She stepped slightly to the side, eyes fixed on the ground near the object. "The dust," she said. "It didn't move correctly."

Bill was already watching.

The next gust came. The dust approached the object and changed—not stopped, not deflected, but reinterpreted. The path bent, not around it but through it, as though the air itself had been reassigned a different relationship to space.

Mercer stared. "That's not possible."

"No," Alex said. "It's consistent."

Bill didn't move, but his attention sharpened.

"That's not environmental," Mercer added. "That's active."

"Yes," Bill said.

The word settled.

Active.

Not just holding stability. Not just reinforcing alignment. Responding.

Alex felt the shift in her thinking. "This isn't just a structure," she said quietly.

Bill nodded. "It's operating."

Mercer looked between them. "Operating implies intent."

Bill didn't answer, because they weren't ready to define that yet.

Alex stepped closer again, just enough to re-enter the stronger field. The clarity returned. The world sharpened.

And then she felt something new.

Not a sound. Not a movement.

A change.

Subtle, but unmistakable.

She stopped. "Bill."

He turned slightly.

"It's different," she said.

He stepped closer, and the moment he crossed into the same threshold, he felt it too—a shift in the field, not instability, but adjustment.

Mercer stepped in beside them. "I don't—" he began, then stopped.

He felt it.

"It's reacting," he said.

No one disagreed.

The object remained still, unchanged, silent, and yet the space around it had altered.

Alex took a slow breath. "We didn't touch it," she said.

"No," Bill replied.

"Then why did it change?"

Bill looked down at the surface, then back out at the terrain. "Because we're here," he said.

That settled heavily.

Mercer shook his head slightly. "That's not enough."

Bill didn't argue, because it was.

They stood in silence for several seconds, not moving, not testing, simply observing.

The field remained stable, but not identical.

Alex stepped back. The change followed, not as strongly, but enough.

"It's tracking proximity," she said.

Bill nodded. "Yes."

Mercer looked uneasy now. "That means it's aware," he said.

Bill didn't respond, because that word carried weight they weren't ready to assign.

Alex looked down at the object again. It still appeared simple—smooth, dark, featureless—but now it felt different. Not just something that existed within the drift, but something that participated in it.

"We need to decide what this is before we interact with it," Mercer said.

Bill nodded. "Yes."

Alex crossed her arms lightly. "We already are interacting with it," she said.

That was the truth. They had entered its field, altered its state, and triggered a response without touching it.

Mercer exhaled slowly. "That's not comforting."

"No," Alex said. "It isn't."

Bill stepped back again. The field eased slightly. The change reduced, but did not disappear.

That was important.

Alex saw it immediately. "It remembers," she said.

Mercer looked at her. "What?"

"The change," she said. "It didn't fully revert."

Bill nodded. "Yes."

That made it worse, because now this wasn't just reactive. It was persistent.

They stood at the edge of the field again, looking at something that should not exist, something that did not belong to the world, and yet defined it.

Alex felt the weight of it settle. "We're not the first ones to find this," she said.

Mercer frowned. "What makes you say that?"

Alex didn't look away. "Because it's already working," she said.

Bill nodded once. "Yes."

That left only one possibility. Someone had built it. Someone had placed it here. And whatever that someone had intended, it was still happening.

The wind moved again across Asterra-9, unchanged, but now it passed through a system they had only just begun to understand.

For the first time, the question wasn't just what the drift was. It was who had designed it to behave this way, and whether they were meant to find out.

Chapter 18 — The Pattern Beneath

They didn't leave the structure immediately. Standing near it felt different—not safer, not exactly, but clearer.

Alex noticed it first in her thinking. The constant background strain, the subtle effort required to interpret space, had eased. It wasn't gone, but it was reduced enough that her thoughts moved more cleanly.

"That's not just physical," she said.

"No," Bill replied.

Mercer shifted slightly, still watching the object. "It's affecting perception. Cognitive load is lower inside the field."

Alex nodded. "Yes." That made it more than a stabilizer.

Bill stepped slowly around the structure, studying it from a different angle. The surface remained unchanged—smooth, dark, and featureless—but the space around it held the real information.

"Look outward," he said.

Alex followed his instruction, not at the structure, but past it. The terrain beyond no longer felt random. It began to resolve—not completely, but enough.

"There's a pattern," she said.

Mercer turned sharply. "Where?"

"Not visually. Structurally. The anchors—they're not just distributed."

Bill nodded. "They're arranged."

Mercer stepped closer to the edge of the field, looking out into the drift. "I'm not seeing a grid."

"It's not a grid," Alex said.

Bill continued moving, adjusting his perspective. "It's relational."

Alex followed his line of thought. The connections became clearer the longer she looked—not lines or coordinates, but distances that held and angles that repeated.

"It's directional," she said.

"Yes," Bill replied.

Mercer frowned. "Directional to what?"

Bill looked down at the structure, then back out across the terrain. "This isn't the center."

Alex felt that immediately. "No," she said. "It isn't." The realization came with quiet certainty. This wasn't the origin. It was part of something larger.

Mercer exhaled slowly. "So we've been working inside a system, and this is just one node."

No one argued.

Alex looked outward again, focusing differently now. If this wasn't the center, then something else was.

"Can you see it?" Mercer asked.

Bill didn't answer immediately. He stepped to the edge of the field, paused, then took one step beyond it. The distortion returned, but this time it felt different—less chaotic, more directional.

Bill adjusted his stance, turning slightly, then again.

"You're following it," Alex said.

"Yes."

"Alignment isn't just local," Bill said.

Alex nodded. "It extends."

He took another step, then another. The movement held—barely, but enough.

Alex stepped out beside him. The shift hit, then settled. Mercer followed more cautiously.

They stood just outside the structure's influence now, but something had changed. The drift no longer felt random. It felt guided.

"Pick a direction," Mercer said.

Bill shook his head. "You don't pick it."

He adjusted slightly. "This way."

Alex felt it immediately—not visually, but in the way the space resisted less. "That holds better," she said.

They moved, not quickly, but with purpose. Each step confirmed the last. Behind them, the structure faded—not physically, but relationally. Alex couldn't place it anymore, but she could still feel it.

"That's wrong," Mercer said.

"No," Bill replied. "It's consistent."

They continued. The terrain shifted, but now it shifted along a direction, not in all directions at once.

After several minutes, Bill stopped. Alex felt it again—a subtle but familiar change.

"Another one," she said.

Bill nodded. Ahead, still not clearly visible, was another point of stability.

Mercer exhaled. "That confirms it."

They moved again, faster now and more certain.

The second structure came into view gradually. Like the first, it shouldn't have been there—same size, same surface, same impossible stillness.

Alex slowed. "That's not coincidence."

"No," Bill said.

Mercer looked between them. "That's design."

No one argued.

They approached carefully. The field engaged before they reached it, and the clarity returned—stronger this time.

Alex stopped. "This one is different."

Bill stepped closer. The space held more tightly. "Yes."

Mercer checked his unit again. "Still no emissions. No energy output. Nothing measurable."

Alex shook her head. "That doesn't matter anymore."

They stood at the edge of the second structure. Two points, connected.

Alex looked back. She couldn't see the first one, but she knew where it was—not by position, but by relationship.

"That's the pattern," she said.

Bill nodded once. "Yes."

Mercer exhaled slowly. "How many of these are there?"

No one answered, because the number was no longer the right question.

Alex looked out across Asterra-9. The drift stretched endlessly, but now it didn't feel empty. It felt structured, layered, intentional.

"This is a network," she said.

Bill nodded. "Yes."

Mercer looked uneasy. "Then we're not exploring a phenomenon."

Alex shook her head. "No."

She looked at the structure, then into the distance. "We're inside something built."

The words settled, and no one spoke, because that changed everything—not just how they moved, but why it existed and what it might do next.

The wind passed across the terrain again, unchanged, but now they understood something they hadn't before. They weren't lost in a broken world. They were moving through a system, and they had just found its pattern.

Which meant somewhere ahead there was a center, and whatever was there was the reason all of this existed.

Chapter 19 — The Direction of the Center

They didn't need to discuss it after the second structure. Two points were enough. Two confirmations. This wasn't random. It wasn't environmental. It wasn't a phenomenon they had wandered into by chance. It was a system, and systems had direction.

Alex stood at the edge of the second structure's field, looking outward. The clarity held stronger here than it had at the first point, but it didn't extend far. Beyond a certain distance, the drift resumed—subtle at first, then increasingly difficult to interpret. But now it no longer felt chaotic. It felt guided.

"We don't search anymore," she said.

Bill glanced at her. "No."

Mercer folded his arms, watching the terrain. "Then we follow it."

Bill nodded once. "Yes."

That was the shift. Not exploration. Not recovery. Pursuit.

Alex took a slow breath and stepped just beyond the edge of the field. The distortion returned immediately, but she was ready for it now. She adjusted, not by sight, but by resistance.

"This way," she said.

Bill watched her for a moment, then nodded. "Yes."

Mercer stepped out after them, less hesitant than before. "That's new," he said.

Alex allowed herself the smallest hint of a smile. "It is."

They moved forward deliberately, not cautiously and not blindly. The direction held, and that was the first confirmation. Each step aligned more easily than the last, not perfectly but consistently.

Behind them, the second structure faded from awareness. It wasn't gone, just no longer usable as a reference. That didn't matter. They weren't navigating by position anymore. They were following relationship.

Bill adjusted slightly. Alex matched him. Mercer followed. The drift shifted around them, but now it shifted along a single axis.

"That's it," Mercer said quietly.

Alex nodded. "It's directional."

Bill didn't speak. He continued forward.

Minutes passed. The terrain remained unchanged to the eye, but the feel of it grew more defined—less resistance, more coherence.

Then Bill stopped.

Alex felt it immediately. It wasn't an anchor. It was something else.

"What is it?" Mercer asked.

Bill didn't answer right away. He turned slightly, then again.

"It's pulling," he said.

Alex felt it too. Not physically, but relationally. The direction they had been following wasn't just stable. It was converging.

"That's new," she said.

"Yes."

Mercer frowned. "I don't like that."

Bill didn't respond, because this was what they had been moving toward.

They advanced again. The pull strengthened—not force, not pressure, but guidance. It felt as if alignment was no longer something they created, but something they were entering.

Alex noticed her breathing had slowed, not intentionally, but naturally.

"That's affecting us," Mercer said.

"Yes," Alex replied.

Bill kept moving. The terrain ahead began to resolve more quickly now, not completely, but enough to suggest structure beyond what they had already seen.

After several more minutes, it appeared. Not suddenly, but gradually.

A third structure.

It was larger than the others, not by much, but enough to matter.

Alex slowed. "That's not the same," she said.

Bill didn't answer. He was already studying it.

The field extended further. The clarity held stronger. And the pull centered on it.

Mercer exhaled slowly. "That's not just another node."

No. It wasn't.

They approached carefully. The field engaged earlier than expected, and Alex felt it immediately. The world sharpened more than before.

"This one is stronger," she said.

Bill nodded. "Yes."

Mercer checked his unit again. "Still nothing measurable. No emissions. No signal."

Alex didn't look at him. "That doesn't matter."

They stopped just outside the structure. It looked the same as the others—smooth, dark, and featureless—but the space around it was different. More controlled. More defined.

Alex took one slow step forward. The shift didn't resist. It accepted.

She stopped. "That's wrong," she said quietly.

Bill stepped beside her. "Yes."

Mercer remained just behind them. "I'm starting to think 'wrong' is the baseline here."

No one disagreed.

Bill studied the structure, then the space beyond it. "It's not the center," he said.

Alex felt that immediately. "No."

Mercer frowned. "Then what is it?"

Bill didn't answer right away, because the answer was becoming clear.

"It's closer," Alex said.

Bill nodded. "Yes."

That was enough. They had direction. They had pattern. They had confirmation. And now they had escalation.

Alex looked past the structure. For the first time, she thought she could sense it—not clearly, not visually, but in the way the space beyond held stronger still.

"There's something further," she said.

Bill didn't look at her. "I know."

Mercer exhaled. "Of course there is."

They stood in silence for a moment, three people at the edge of something they had only just begun to understand, and already it was leading them somewhere.

Alex drew in a slow breath. "We keep going," she said.

Bill nodded. "Yes."

There was no hesitation, no debate—only continuation.

Because now they weren't searching for survivors, and they weren't mapping the system.

They were following it.

And whatever lay at the center, it already knew the way.

The wind moved across Asterra-9 again, unchanged, but now it moved across something ordered, something deliberate, something that had been waiting for someone to follow it far enough.

And they just had.

Chapter 20 — Too Close

They didn't move immediately after reaching the third structure. Something about it had changed the pace—not physically, but internally. Alex felt it first as hesitation. It wasn't fear and it wasn't uncertainty. It was a quiet recognition that they were no longer just observing the system. They were approaching something within it.

"This is where it changes," she said.

Bill didn't answer. He was looking past the structure, not at what was in front of them, but at what came next.

Mercer shifted uneasily behind them. "We've already gone further than we should have."

Alex glanced back at him. "We passed that point a while ago."

"That's not reassuring."

"It's not meant to be."

Bill stepped forward, just one step. The field responded immediately—stronger than before. It didn't resist. It adjusted.

Alex felt it at once. The space didn't just stabilize. It tightened.

"Bill," she said.

He stopped.

"What is it?" he asked.

She looked around carefully. The clarity had increased again, but not in the same way as before. It wasn't just easier to perceive. It was more defined. Edges where there hadn't been edges. Boundaries where there hadn't been boundaries.

"This is different," she said.

"Yes," Bill replied.

Mercer stepped closer. "I feel that. That's not just stabilization."

No, it wasn't.

Bill took another step. This time the response came faster. The field shifted around them, not broadly, but precisely.

Alex's breath caught. "It's focusing."

Bill didn't move.

Mercer stepped back one pace, and the effect lessened immediately. "That's proximity-based," he said.

"Yes," Alex replied.

Bill stood at the edge of something, not visible, but unmistakably present. Alex stepped forward to match him, and the effect returned stronger. She felt it in her chest, a pressure not physical but relational, as if the space itself were narrowing.

"This is a boundary," she said.

Bill nodded.

Mercer shook his head slightly. "That's not how boundaries work."

"No," Alex said. "It isn't."

But that didn't change what it was.

Bill looked down briefly, then back up. "It's limiting access."

That settled heavily.

"Why?" Mercer asked.

Bill didn't answer, because they all understood.

They were too close.

Alex looked past the structure again. The sense of direction was still there—stronger now, more defined. Whatever lay ahead was pulling them in.

But the system was pushing back.

"We need to decide," Mercer said.

"Decide what?" Alex asked.

"How far we go."

That was the question—not whether they could continue, but whether they should.

Bill stepped forward again. The response was immediate and stronger. The space tightened further.

Alex felt it clearly now. This wasn't just guidance anymore. It was control.

"Bill, stop."

He did.

The pressure eased, though not completely.

Mercer let out a breath. "That answers that."

Alex shook her head slightly. "No. It confirms something."

She looked at Bill. "This isn't just a system."

"No," he said.

"It's regulating access."

"Yes."

Mercer folded his arms. "Which means there's something ahead it doesn't want us reaching."

Bill didn't respond, because that assumption might not be correct.

Alex saw it. "You don't think it's stopping us."

Bill shook his head. "No."

"Then what?"

He looked back toward the unseen direction. "It's testing us."

That landed harder.

Mercer frowned. "That's worse."

"Yes," Alex said quietly.

Testing implied criteria. And criteria implied something that decided.

Bill stepped back. The pressure eased further. The boundary relaxed, but it did not disappear.

Alex noticed immediately. "It stays."

"Yes," Bill replied.

Persistent, like everything else in the system.

Mercer looked between them. "So what do we do?"

Alex didn't answer right away. She looked at the structure, then beyond it, then back at Bill.

"We don't push through," she said.

Bill nodded. "No."

Mercer blinked. "That's a first."

Alex allowed a faint smile. "We learn first."

That was the shift. Not forward. Not retreat. Understanding.

Bill stepped slightly to the side. The pressure changed, not reduced, but adjusted.

Alex saw it immediately. "You're mapping the boundary."

"Yes."

Mercer stepped closer again, carefully. "We can define it."

"Yes."

That gave them something new—not just direction, but control. Limited, but real.

They moved slowly along the edge, testing, adjusting, learning. The boundary responded not randomly, but consistently.

After several minutes, Bill stopped. The direction ahead was still there, stronger than ever, waiting.

But now they understood something they hadn't before. This wasn't just a path.

It was a threshold.

And crossing it would change everything.

Alex drew in a slow breath. "We're not ready."

Bill nodded. "No."

Mercer exhaled. "That might be the smartest thing we've said all day."

No one disagreed.

They stood there a moment longer at the edge of something that was beginning to define them as much as they were defining it.

Then Bill turned. "Back."

Alex nodded. "Yes."

It wasn't retreat.

It was preparation.

Because now they knew where they were going.

And that meant the next time they came here, they would not be guessing.

The wind moved across Asterra-9 again, unchanged, but now they had found something the world did not give freely.

A limit.

And whatever lay beyond it was waiting.

Chapter 21 — Preparing to Cross

They didn't speak much on the way back, not because there was nothing to say, but because everything that mattered had already been said. The path back to the second structure held more easily now. Not perfectly, but with enough consistency that each step required less correction than before. The anchors, once discovered, felt more accessible and more reliable.

Alex noticed it immediately. "We're moving faster," she said.

Bill nodded once. "Yes."

Mercer followed just behind them, glancing at his unit before lowering it again. "I still can't track it," he said. "But I can feel it now. That's… new."

"That's the shift," Alex replied. "We're not trying to measure it anymore."

"No," Bill said. "We're working with it."

They reached the second structure without incident. The field engaged around them, and clarity returned in a controlled, familiar way. Behind them, farther back along the path, the first structure remained out of view, but not out of mind.

Mercer stepped fully into the field and exhaled. "I'm starting to understand why this works," he said.

"Then say it," Alex replied.

He hesitated briefly, organizing the thought. "It reduces uncertainty. Not just spatially, but cognitively. It narrows the number of possible interpretations the brain has to process."

Alex nodded. "Yes."

Bill remained still, but his silence suggested agreement.

Mercer looked toward the boundary. "If that's what it does, then crossing that threshold means losing that reduction."

"It means entering a space with higher demand," Alex said.

"Yes," Bill added.

They stood in silence for a moment, not uncertain and not unprepared, but aware. The next move would not be like the others.

Alex turned slightly toward Bill. "What changes?" she asked.

Bill didn't answer immediately. He looked out across the terrain, then back at the structure beneath their feet. "Everything past the boundary is less stable," he said, "but not randomly."

"More selective," Alex said.

Bill nodded.

Mercer frowned. "Selective how?"

Bill met his gaze. "It doesn't respond the same way to everything."

That settled heavily.

Alex crossed her arms lightly. "So the system distinguishes."

"Yes."

"Based on what?"

Bill didn't answer, because that was what they were about to find out.

Mercer let out a slow breath. "I don't like entering a system where we don't understand the criteria."

Alex almost smiled. "That puts you in a very large category."

He didn't return it.

"Then we define as much as we can before we cross," he said.

Bill nodded. "Yes."

That became the plan. Not guesswork. Not reaction. Preparation.

They began testing immediately. Bill moved to the edge of the field and stepped just outside it. The shift returned, sharp and immediate. He adjusted, held, then stepped back.

Alex followed, repeating the movement. The difference was clearer now, not just instability, but variation—subtle changes depending on how she moved, where she placed her weight, and how she oriented herself.

"It's not just position," she said.

"No," Bill replied.

Mercer stepped forward more cautiously. "Then what else?"

Bill looked at Alex. "Consistency."

That word landed.

Alex felt it settle into place. Not just where you were, but how you held yourself within it.

She stepped forward again, slower this time, more deliberate. The shift responded, but less violently.

"That's it," she said.

"Yes."

Mercer tried the same. At first he overcorrected; the distortion spiked, then eased as he adjusted. "I see it," he said. "It reacts to instability."

"Yes," Alex said.

"Not just spatial instability," Bill added.

Mercer nodded slowly. "Behavioral."

That made it worse, because now they weren't just navigating space. They were being evaluated.

Alex looked toward the unseen direction again. "So the boundary isn't just distance."

"No," Bill said.

"It's a filter."

Silence followed.

Mercer ran a hand along the back of his neck. "I really don't like that word."

"No," Alex said. "Neither do I."

But it fit.

They continued testing, step, adjust, pause, repeat, each pass revealing a little more. The system wasn't random. It wasn't arbitrary. It responded consistently.

Alex stepped back into the field and exhaled. "We can do this."

Bill looked at her. "Yes."

Mercer remained near the edge, watching the boundary. "We can," he said, then added, "That doesn't mean we should."

Alex didn't answer immediately, because that was also true.

Bill turned toward the direction they had been following. "We go," he said.

Not now, but soon.

That distinction mattered.

Alex nodded. "Yes."

Preparation first. Then crossing.

Mercer let out a slow breath. "If we're going through that," he said, "we do it right."

Bill nodded. "Yes."

They stood together for a moment longer, three people at the edge of something that would not allow mistakes. For the first time since they had arrived, they were ready to face it, not because they understood it completely, but because they understood enough.

Alex looked out across Asterra-9. The drift no longer felt like an unknown threat. It felt like a system with rules, structure, and limits. And just beyond those limits, something waited.

The wind moved across the terrain again, unchanged, but now they knew the difference between where they could stand and where they were about to go.

And soon, they would cross that line.

Chapter 22 — Crossing the Threshold

They didn't delay. Not after everything they had confirmed, and not after the boundary had revealed itself. Preparation had done what it could. Now they had to cross.

Bill stood at the edge of the field, just inside the stability of the second structure. Alex and Mercer stood with him, each aware that what lay ahead was not simply more of the same. This was different. This was the point where the system would decide whether they belonged.

"Same method," Bill said.

Alex nodded. "Controlled movement. No overcorrection."

Mercer exhaled slowly. "And no assumptions."

Bill glanced at him. "Yes."

They stepped forward together. The shift hit immediately, stronger than before, sharper and more defined.

Alex felt it as pressure, not against her body, but against her sense of position. The world didn't just loosen around them. It resisted.

She adjusted, not quickly, but carefully. The pressure eased slightly. "That's it," she said.

Bill moved again, one step, then another. Alex matched him. Mercer followed, more controlled now than before. The system responded not violently, but precisely. Each movement was met with a counterbalance, an adjustment that either allowed them forward or forced correction.

"It's evaluating us," Mercer said quietly.

Bill didn't respond. They already knew.

They continued forward. The boundary did not disappear. It extended.

Alex felt it clearly now. This wasn't a line they crossed. It was a condition they entered.

"Stay consistent," she said.

Bill nodded.

They moved steadily, deliberately, and with control. The pressure increased again, not overwhelming, but intentional.

Alex slowed her breathing, forcing her movement into a measured rhythm. Every instinct told her to correct faster, but that only made it worse. "Don't fight it," she said.

Mercer adjusted immediately. "That helps."

Bill stepped forward again. The space shifted, then aligned.

They were through.

Not completely, but enough.

Alex felt it the moment it changed. The pressure didn't vanish. It stabilized.

"This is different," she said.

Bill looked ahead. "Yes."

They stopped for the first time since crossing. Behind them, the second structure was no longer a usable reference. Ahead, the drift no longer behaved the same way. It held, not like the anchors and not like the structures, but consistently.

Mercer looked around slowly. "This is… stable."

Alex shook her head. "No."

She took a careful step. The space held, then adjusted, then held again. "It's conditional."

Bill nodded. "Yes."

That was the difference. This wasn't a place. It was a state.

Mercer exhaled. "That's worse."

"Yes," Alex said, because now the system wasn't just guiding them. It was requiring something from them.

Bill looked forward again. The direction was still there, stronger now and more defined. They hadn't lost it. They had aligned with it.

"That way," he said.

Alex felt it, not visually, but unmistakably.

They moved, not because it was safe, but because it was clear.

The terrain ahead began to resolve more quickly than before. The distortions still existed, but now they followed a pattern that could be anticipated.

"That's new," Mercer said.

Alex nodded. "We're inside it now."

Bill kept moving. The pull strengthened, not as force, but as direction. The system had shifted from resisting them to guiding them.

After several minutes, something began to resolve ahead. Not sharply and not fully, but enough.

A structure.

Larger than the others.

Further away, but unmistakable.

Alex slowed. "That's it," she said.

Bill didn't answer. He already knew.

Mercer stared. "That's not just another node."

No, it wasn't.

The scale was different. The presence was different. Even at a distance, it held more strongly than anything they had encountered.

Alex felt it, not as pressure, but as weight. "We found it," she said.

Bill nodded once. "Yes."

There was no excitement and no relief. Only recognition.

Because this was what everything had been leading to.

They stood there for a moment, aligned within a system they had only just begun to understand, and now they were looking at its center.

The wind moved across Asterra-9 again, unchanged, but now they stood beyond the boundary, inside the structure.

And whatever had built this place was no longer hidden.

It was waiting.

And they were coming.

Chapter 23 — The Center

They did not speak for several moments after they saw it. At first, that was because there was nothing useful to say. Language lagged behind the sight of it. Then it became something else—recognition. Not of what it was, but of what it meant.

The structure ahead was larger than the others by enough to matter. Not massive in the sense of a tower or a building, but unmistakably central. It sat low against the terrain, dark and smooth like the other nodes, yet carried a different weight in the way the space around it behaved. The drift did not merely ease near it. It organized itself.

Alex felt that difference before she could define it. The world ahead no longer seemed to resist interpretation. It resolved in layers, each one settling into place more firmly than the last, as though the space around the structure had a stronger claim on reality than anything beyond it.

"That's the center," she said quietly.

Bill did not answer immediately. He stood very still, studying not just the structure but the field around it, the way the terrain aligned toward it and the way every shift they had followed now seemed to converge there.

Finally he said, "Yes."

Mercer let out a breath that sounded almost like disbelief. "It's too symmetrical," he said. "The way everything leads here. That's not natural."

No one argued, because by now nothing about Asterra-9 could honestly be mistaken for natural.

They moved forward carefully, not with the uncertainty of earlier steps and not with the speed of panic. This was something else—a controlled approach toward a place they already knew would matter more than anything else they had found. The system did not resist them now, and that, more than anything, unsettled Alex.

It allowed them forward.

"You feel that?" Mercer asked.

"Yes," Alex said.

Bill gave a short nod.

The space around them had changed again. The pressure that had marked the boundary was gone. The corrective resistance that had forced them into alignment had eased. In its place was a strange, deliberate clarity, as though the system had completed its evaluation and chosen not to interfere.

That was not comfort. It was invitation, and invitation could be more dangerous than refusal.

The center resolved further as they approached. Its surface carried the same impossible smoothness as the smaller structures, but now faint lines could be seen beneath the dark finish, curves so subtle they vanished when looked at directly, only to reappear at the edge of vision. They did not seem carved or damaged. They seemed inherent, as though the object had been formed with layers too fine for ordinary perception to hold all at once.

Alex slowed. "There's detail in it," she said.

Bill nodded once. "Yes."

Mercer lifted his unit, then lowered it again almost immediately. "Still nothing useful," he muttered. "No signal, no energy reading, no thermal variation. It's like the thing refuses to exist in measurable terms."

"It exists," Alex said.

Mercer looked at the center again. "Unfortunately, yes."

They stopped several paces from it. This close, the effect on the surrounding space was undeniable. Everything held more tightly here. Angles resolved. Distances stopped slipping. The world felt less like a fractured field of probabilities and more like a place.

Alex exhaled slowly. "This is what the other nodes were doing, just at a smaller level."

Bill remained focused on the structure itself. "No."

She looked at him. "No?"

"The others stabilized movement," he said. "This does more."

Mercer frowned. "How can you tell?"

Bill took one step to the side. The effect changed instantly, not enough to destabilize them, but enough to reveal that the clarity here was not uniform. It deepened in some positions and loosened in others, all in relation to the center.

Alex saw it too. "It's shaping the field," she said.

Bill nodded. "Yes."

That was worse, because shaping implied design, and design implied intention far more strongly than any strange natural anomaly ever could.

Mercer studied the space around them with renewed unease. "So this isn't just the strongest node. It's controlling the others."

Bill did not answer, but he didn't need to. Every path they had followed, every anchor, every transition point—everything had pointed here.

Alex felt the truth of it settle into place. "This is the baseline," she said. "The rest of the system is being referenced against this."

"Yes," Bill said.

Mercer gave a small shake of his head. "I would have preferred this world to remain mysterious in a less organized way."

Alex almost smiled, but the expression never fully formed. "I know."

For several seconds, no one moved. The wind crossed the plain beyond them, but inside the center's field it seemed strangely muted, as though even air behaved with more discipline here.

Then Bill stepped closer.

Alex tensed immediately. "Bill."

He stopped, but did not step back. "It's not reacting the same way as the others."

"That does not make it safe."

"No," he said. "It doesn't."

Mercer moved up beside Alex. "I'd like to be on record as strongly supporting not touching the alien control structure in the middle of the impossible spatial field."

"That is an excellent position," Alex said.

Bill said nothing. He was still watching the surface.

Then the center changed.

Not physically and not dramatically, but unmistakably. The faint lines beneath the dark surface became more visible, not because they brightened, but because the space around them clarified even further. Shapes that had previously been too subtle to resolve now began to separate from one another in precise, concentric patterns.

Alex felt her pulse jump. "It's responding."

Mercer took one step back. "That's bad."

Bill didn't move. He was studying it.

"No," he said quietly. "It noticed us."

That did not sound better.

The lines continued to emerge, not glowing and not opening, but aligning, like a hidden geometry revealing itself in answer to proximity.

Alex watched the patterns spread across the surface and felt a cold realization form. “It isn’t waking up,” she said.

Bill glanced at her.

“It’s already awake.”

Mercer’s silence after that was more telling than any reply.

The center’s field shifted again. This time the change ran through the space beneath their feet. Not enough to throw them off balance, but enough that Alex felt a subtle realignment pass through the ground and into her sense of position. It was as though the structure were comparing them against something, measuring, sorting, deciding.

She looked at Bill. He had felt it too. “Still think it’s testing us?” she asked.

“Yes.”

Mercer’s voice was tighter now. “Testing for what?”

Bill looked at the structure, then out across the terrain they had crossed to reach it. “Compatibility,” he said.

The word landed heavily, because it explained too much. Why the boundary had resisted, why consistency mattered, why careless movement had made things worse. This system was not merely dangerous. It was selective.

Alex crossed her arms lightly, not from comfort but to steady herself against the thought. “So the drift isn’t just a field,” she said. “It’s a filter built around this.”

Bill nodded once.

Mercer stared at the center. “A filter for what?”

This time, Bill did hesitate. Not because he had no thought, but because he likely had too many. When he finally spoke, his voice remained as steady as ever.

"For access."

No one answered right away, because they were already standing inside the implications.

The center had not hidden itself from them. It had led them here—through nodes, through anchors, through the boundary. Not easily and not freely, but deliberately.

That realization changed the feel of the entire world in an instant. Asterra-9 was not merely hazardous terrain wrapped around a mystery. It was an approach, a process, a controlled sequence of conditions designed to bring someone eventually to this exact place.

Alex felt the weight of that settle more deeply than the sight of the center itself. "This wasn't built to keep people away," she said softly.

Bill looked at her. "No."

She held his gaze. "It was built to decide who gets through."

"Yes."

Mercer let out a thin breath. "I'm finding that only marginally more comforting."

"It shouldn't be comforting at all," Alex said.

"No," he admitted. "Fair point."

The surface patterns stabilized. Now that they had fully emerged, they no longer shifted. They formed nested arcs and intersecting lines too precise to be accidental and too structured to be decorative. Alex had the uncomfortable sense that, if she stared long enough, she might begin to understand them, and that understanding them might change something.

She looked away first.

“We need to decide what this is before we do anything else,” Mercer said.

Bill shook his head slightly. “No.”

Alex frowned. “No?”

“We already know what it is,” he said.

Mercer looked at him. “Then I’d love to hear it.”

Bill’s eyes returned to the center. “It’s a gate,” he said.

Silence followed, longer than before, not because the word was unclear, but because it was too clear.

Alex looked back at the center, really looked at it. The layered geometry, the controlled field, the filtering process around it, and the network of smaller nodes guiding movement inward all aligned with that single idea. The word fit too well.

Not a door in any ordinary sense and not something with hinges or seams, but a threshold, a mechanism for transition, a point of passage.

All at once, the entire structure of Asterra-9 rearranged itself in her mind. The drift was not the anomaly. The drift was the approach. The world itself had been shaped around a center meant to be reached only under specific conditions.

“A gate to where?” Mercer asked.

Bill answered with rare honesty. “I don’t know.”

That, somehow, made it more real.

They stood there in the center’s field with the wind moving softly across the plain beyond, three human beings at the edge of something built for purposes older than any of them understood.

Alex felt fear, yes, but something else as well—not wonder exactly, but recognition. They had crossed out of rescue and into discovery a while ago, but this was the first true answer the world had given them.

And like most true answers, it had only made the deeper questions larger.

She looked at Bill. "What now?"

He didn't answer at once.

Then he said, "Now we learn what opens it."

Mercer closed his eyes briefly. "I was afraid you were going to say that."

Alex kept her eyes on the center. "So was I."

The center remained still, silent, and present—no longer hidden and no longer deniable.

Whatever had built Asterra-9 had not built a broken world.

It had built a way through.

And Bill, Alex, and Mercer were standing at the end of it.

Or perhaps only at the beginning.

Chapter 24 — What Opens It

They didn't approach it immediately. Even after naming it, even after understanding what it likely was, the risk hadn't changed. Alex kept her distance, studying the surface again, this time not just as an object, but as a system waiting for input. Because that was what it had to be. A gate did not simply exist. It responded.

"If this is a threshold," Mercer said, "then it requires something to activate it."

Bill didn't answer right away. He was watching the patterns, not just seeing them, but following them.

Alex noticed that. "You're tracking something."

Bill nodded once. "Yes."

"What?"

He didn't look away from the surface. "They're not static."

Mercer frowned. "They look static."

"They're not."

Alex stepped slightly to the side. The lines shifted, not dramatically, but enough. She narrowed her focus. "You're right. They're changing relative to position."

Bill nodded. "They respond to alignment."

That fit. Everything here responded to alignment.

Mercer crossed his arms. "So this thing doesn't open with a button."

"No," Alex said. "It opens with a condition."

That was worse, because conditions could be misunderstood or failed.

Bill stepped closer. Alex didn't stop him this time, because stopping him wouldn't answer anything. The patterns shifted again, more clearly now. Lines that had seemed disconnected began to resolve into arcs, arcs into intersections, intersections into something almost coherent.

"Coherent," Alex said quietly.

Bill nodded. "Yes."

Mercer looked between them. "I'm not seeing it."

"You will," Alex said. "You just need to stop looking at it as an object."

"And start?"

"As a relationship."

That took a moment.

Then Mercer exhaled. "I hate that you're right."

Alex almost smiled.

Bill didn't. He moved again, not randomly, but following. The lines shifted more strongly now, not reacting but aligning.

Alex felt it immediately. "This is directional."

"Yes," Bill said.

Mercer stepped closer. "Directional how?"

Bill adjusted his stance. The pattern changed, subtly but clearly.

"It's not just responding to position," Alex said. "It's responding to orientation."

Bill looked at her. "Yes."

That was the key. Not where they stood, but how they stood.

Mercer shook his head slowly. "That's not intuitive."

"No," Alex said. "It's intentional."

That settled it. This wasn't meant to be easy. It was meant to be correct.

Bill shifted again. The arcs tightened. The intersections became clearer. Alex stepped beside him, matching his angle. The pattern sharpened.

"That's it," she said.

Mercer watched carefully. "You're aligning with it."

"Yes."

Not controlling. Not activating. Matching.

Alex felt it deepen. The space around them held more firmly. The clarity intensified, not just in the environment, but in the structure itself. The surface was no longer featureless. It was becoming readable—not fully, but enough.

Mercer took another step forward. "Something's happening."

"Yes," Alex replied.

Bill didn't move. He held the alignment. The pattern continued to resolve, then stopped.

Not completed.

Paused.

Alex felt it immediately. "It's waiting."

Bill nodded. "Yes."

Mercer looked between them. "For what?"

That was the question. Not how it worked, but what it required.

Alex studied the pattern again. Something was missing, not visually, but relationally.

"This isn't enough," she said.

Bill didn't disagree. "No."

Mercer exhaled. "Of course it's not."

Alex stepped back slightly. The pattern loosened, but didn't disappear. That mattered.

"It holds partial alignment," she said.

Bill nodded. "Yes."

"So we're not starting over each time."

"No."

Mercer looked relieved—for about half a second. "I'll take that."

Alex looked back at the structure. "If this is a gate, then alignment is only part of the requirement."

Bill nodded. "Yes."

Mercer frowned. "What else?"

Bill didn't answer, because they hadn't seen it yet.

Alex looked out across the terrain, back the way they had come, then forward again. "There's more to the system than just position," she said.

Bill followed her gaze. "Yes."

The realization came slowly, then all at once.

"This isn't just spatial," she said. "It's contextual."

Bill nodded.

Mercer closed his eyes briefly. "I really don't like where this is going."

Alex didn't either, because now they weren't just aligning physically. They might need to align with something else.

Bill stepped back. The pattern dimmed slightly. Not gone. Waiting.

Alex crossed her arms lightly. "We're missing a variable."

Bill nodded. "Yes."

Mercer looked between them. "Then we find it."

Alex shook her head. "No."

He frowned. "No?"

She looked at the structure again. "It finds us."

That changed the tone immediately.

Bill didn't disagree, because everything they had seen suggested the same thing. This system didn't just respond. It evaluated.

And now it was waiting for something they hadn't yet provided.

The wind moved across the plain again, unchanged. But inside the center's field, nothing was still. Everything was poised, ready.

And whatever this gate required, they were about to find out.

Chapter 25 — The Missing Variable

They didn't move right away. Standing in front of the center, with its surface partially resolved and waiting, felt different than anything they had encountered so far. It wasn't unstable, and it wasn't resisting. It was incomplete.

Alex kept her eyes on the structure, replaying what they had already confirmed. Alignment mattered. Orientation mattered. Consistency mattered. But none of it had been enough. "It's not just position," she said quietly.

"No," Bill replied.

Mercer folded his arms, watching both of them. "And it's not just movement. We already tested that."

Alex nodded. "Yes." That narrowed it. They had accounted for where they stood, how they moved, and how they held alignment. What remained was not external.

Alex exhaled slowly. "It's us."

Mercer frowned. "I'm going to need more detail than that."

Bill finally shifted his attention toward her. "Explain."

Alex didn't rush. Everything here had punished quick conclusions. "The system doesn't just respond to what we do," she said. "It responds to how we do it."

Mercer tilted his head slightly. "That's… not new."

"No," Alex said. "But we've been treating it like a mechanical condition." She gestured toward the structure. "It isn't."

Bill watched her closely now.

"It's evaluating consistency," she continued. "Not just in movement, but in intent."

Silence followed.

Mercer blinked. "I'm not sure I like the word intent showing up in a system like this."

Alex didn't either, but it fit.

Bill turned back toward the center. "That explains the boundary."

Alex nodded. "Yes. Not just filtering movement—filtering behavior."

Mercer ran a hand along the back of his neck. "That's a very uncomfortable distinction."

"Yes," Alex said, because now they weren't just navigating a space. They were being measured.

Bill stepped forward slightly. The pattern responded, not fully, but more than before.

Alex watched carefully. "What changed?" Mercer asked.

Bill didn't answer right away. He was holding still, not just physically, but deliberately.

Alex felt it—the difference. "He's not adjusting," she said.

Mercer frowned. "That's what we've been doing the whole time."

"Yes," Alex said. "And that might be the problem."

Bill didn't move. The pattern sharpened slightly, not complete, but closer.

Alex stepped forward beside him. This time she didn't match his movement. She matched his stillness.

The shift responded more clearly. "That's it," she said quietly.

Mercer watched closely. "You're… not correcting."

"Yes," Alex replied. "We're holding."

Bill nodded once. The pattern deepened. Lines that had previously resisted alignment now settled more cleanly into place.

Mercer stepped forward more cautiously and tried to replicate it. At first nothing changed. Then he stilled, not just stopping movement, but letting the need to adjust drop. The pattern responded again, stronger.

Mercer exhaled. "That's not comfortable."

"No," Alex said, because everything they had learned so far had depended on correction, adjustment, and control, and now the system required something else.

Bill spoke quietly. "It's not just alignment."

Alex nodded. "It's trust."

That word settled into the space between them.

Mercer shook his head slightly. "I was hoping it wasn't going to be that."

Alex almost smiled, but didn't, because it was exactly that.

They stood there together, not correcting, not adjusting, simply holding. The pattern responded steadily. The arcs resolved further. The intersections aligned. The surface of the center became clearer than it had ever been, not fully open, but closer.

Alex felt it. "This is what it was waiting for," she said.

Bill nodded. "Yes."

Mercer looked between them. "So the missing variable is… what?"

Alex didn't hesitate this time. "Consistency without resistance."

Bill added quietly, "Alignment without control."

Mercer let out a slow breath. "That's not something you can fake."

"No," Alex said. "It isn't."

That was the point. This wasn't a system you could force. It was one you had to meet on its own terms.

The pattern held, stronger now and more complete. Still waiting, but no longer distant.

Alex looked at the center, then at Bill. "We're close."

Bill nodded. "Yes."

Mercer glanced between them. "And the next step?"

Bill didn't answer right away, because they all knew what it was. Not another adjustment. Not another test. A decision.

Alex felt it settle. "We stop trying to solve it," she said.

Bill nodded. "And we let it resolve."

Mercer closed his eyes briefly. "I really hope that works."

Alex didn't respond, because hope wasn't part of this system. Only alignment. Only consistency. Only truth.

The wind moved across the plain again, unchanged. But inside the center's field, everything was closer than it had been before. The pattern held, waiting.

And this time, they understood what it was waiting for.

Chapter 26 — The Opening

They didn't move. That was the first requirement they understood, and the hardest to maintain.

Standing before the center, with the pattern nearly resolved and the structure holding in a state that felt both complete and unfinished, demanded something different from anything they had done before. Not action. Not adjustment. Stillness.

Alex focused on her breathing, not to control it, but to keep it from becoming something she would try to control. Every instinct she had built through training pushed toward correction, toward doing something, fixing something, improving something. But this was not something to fix.

Beside her, Bill held the same posture, not rigid and not forced, but steady in a way that felt deliberate without being strained. Mercer stood just behind them, quieter than Alex had ever seen him. For once, he wasn't trying to measure or interpret. He was holding.

The pattern responded, not all at once and not dramatically, but steadily. Lines that had hovered just out of clarity began to settle into place. The arcs resolved further, intersections tightening into forms that felt less abstract and more intentional. Alex didn't try to follow them. She let them be.

"That's it," Mercer said quietly. "It's moving."

"No," Alex replied just as quietly. "It's resolving."

Bill didn't speak, but she felt the agreement.

The surface of the center shifted, not physically and not in the way a door opens or a machine activates, but in the way a concept becomes clear after being just out of reach. The patterns were no longer incomplete. They were aligning, and they were aligning with them.

Alex felt the moment it changed, not as a sound or a motion, but as recognition. The system had stopped waiting.

The lines across the surface completed their paths, forming a structure that no longer felt partial. The arcs met, the intersections held, and the entire surface of the center became something that could finally be understood, not in detail, but in function.

Bill spoke softly. "It's ready."

Mercer exhaled slowly. "I'm not sure that makes me feel better."

Alex didn't answer, because she felt it too.

The space around them shifted again, but this time it wasn't testing. It was allowing.

The center didn't open; it revealed. The dark surface that had held its form so tightly began to change, not by separating or breaking, but by becoming something else. The smoothness gave way to depth, as though what had been solid now extended beyond what their eyes could measure.

Alex felt a pull, not physical or forceful, but relational.

"That's new," Mercer said.

"Yes," Bill replied.

The pull didn't increase. It clarified.

Alex understood it then. "It's not pulling us in."

Bill glanced at her.

"It's showing us the path."

Mercer let out a quiet breath. "That's somehow worse."

Alex almost smiled, because it was.

The center now appeared less like an object and more like a space, a depth that hadn't been visible before, a presence that suggested transition rather than containment. Everything about it aligned with what they had already begun to understand. This wasn't a door. It was a passage.

Bill took one step forward. Alex felt the system respond immediately, not with resistance or pressure, but with confirmation. The alignment held. He stopped, not out of hesitation, but out of understanding.

Alex stepped beside him. This time, the shift did not challenge her. It accepted her position.

Mercer followed more slowly, but with the same controlled stillness they had learned to maintain. "This is it," he said.

"Yes," Bill replied.

There was no uncertainty, no correction, only continuation.

They stood at the edge of the revealed space, the center no longer hidden and no longer incomplete. Everything they had learned, every adjustment, every realization, every moment of resisting the instinct to force control, had led them here.

Alex looked at Bill. "What happens if we go through?"

Bill didn't answer immediately. He was looking into the depth of the center, studying something that could not yet be fully seen. "I don't know," he said.

That was the truth.

Mercer exhaled. "Finally. Something honest."

Alex kept her eyes on the opening. "We're not guessing anymore."

Bill nodded. "No."

They weren't. They had aligned. They had been accepted. They had reached the point the system had been guiding them toward from the beginning.

Now the next step wasn't about understanding. It was about choice.

The wind moved across Asterra-9 again, unchanged, as if none of this had altered the surface of the world at all. But here, at the center, everything had changed.

Alex took one final breath, then looked at both of them. "We go together."

Bill nodded once. "Yes."

Mercer gave a small, tight smile. "I was hoping you'd say that."

They stepped forward, not cautiously and not blindly, but together.

And the center accepted them, not with sound or motion, but with certainty.

The moment they crossed the threshold, the world behind them did not vanish. It remained, but it no longer held them.

And whatever lay ahead was waiting.

Chapter 27 — Beyond the Gate

The transition was not what Alex expected. There was no flash of light, no sense of acceleration, and no disorientation. One moment they stood at the center of Asterra-9, and the next they were somewhere else.

The ground beneath them felt solid in a way that required no interpretation. There was no shifting, no relational instability, and no need to constantly adjust. Space held completely. Alex took a slow breath and realized almost immediately what was different. She didn't have to think about where she was.

"It's stable," Mercer said, his voice quieter than usual.

"Yes," Bill replied.

Not conditionally stable. Not relatively stable. Absolute.

Alex looked around carefully. The environment was simple, more so than she expected. A wide, open expanse stretched in every direction, flat and unbroken. The surface beneath them appeared almost stone-like, smooth but not artificial in the way the earlier structures had been. Above them, the sky held a soft, diffuse light with no visible source, no sun, no stars, just illumination.

"It's not a planet," Mercer said.

"No," Alex replied.

Bill didn't speak. He was looking ahead.

At first, Alex saw nothing. Then she did.

A structure.

Not like the others.

This one rose vertically from the ground, tall enough to dominate the horizon without overwhelming it. Its surface carried the same dark, smooth quality as the nodes, but here the faint lines were fully visible, clear, precise, and unmistakably intentional.

They moved toward it, not quickly and not cautiously, but naturally. There was no resistance here, no correction, and no need to adjust. The system they had crossed no longer constrained them, or perhaps it had already decided.

Alex felt that thought settle but didn't speak it.

As they approached, the structure resolved further. The lines across its surface were not random markings; they formed patterns that repeated and expanded, like a language built from geometry instead of sound. Mercer slowed slightly.

"This is… readable," he said.

"Yes," Alex replied.

Not in words and not in symbols she could translate, but in structure.

Bill stopped several paces from the base. Alex and Mercer stopped with him. For a moment, no one spoke.

Then the structure responded.

The lines did not flare or brighten. They settled.

What had been in motion slowed, then resolved with a clarity that removed all uncertainty. The patterns no longer shifted in search of alignment. They held, complete and unchanging, as if the structure had reached a conclusion it had been waiting for.

Alex felt it immediately. Not relief. Not victory.

Completion.

Beside her, Mercer exhaled slowly, the tension in his posture easing without fully leaving. "That's new," he said quietly.

Bill did not answer. He was watching the structure with a focus that had shifted from analysis to recognition.

The surface remained still. No further changes came. No new patterns emerged.

For the first time since they had entered the system, nothing was asking anything of them.

Alex became aware of the silence. Not the absence of sound, but the absence of demand. The environment no longer pressed against them. It no longer measured, corrected, or responded.

"It's done," she said.

Bill nodded slightly. "Yes."

Mercer glanced around the open expanse. "So what now?"

Bill's answer was quiet. "Now we see what it was for."

The structure did not move again.

But something else had changed.

Alex felt it before she saw it. A shift in awareness, subtle but unmistakable, as if the space around them had deepened rather than altered. She turned slightly, her eyes scanning the open ground beyond the structure.

At first, there was nothing.

Then there was.

A small figure stood several paces away, positioned just beyond the edge of the structure's base. It had not approached. It had not arrived. It was simply present, as though it had always been there and only now had become visible to them.

Mercer's posture tightened instantly, though he did not raise his weapon. His training held him still.

Bill did not move.

Alex felt no surge of fear. Only a quiet, steady awareness.

The figure was slight, no taller than a young adolescent, with a smooth form that seemed almost too simple to belong in a place built with such precision. Its surface carried a faint, soft luminosity, not enough to illuminate the space, but enough to distinguish it clearly from the environment around it. Its eyes were large and reflective, not sharp, not probing, but attentive.

It watched them.

Not as a threat.

As a presence.

For a long moment, no one spoke.

Then the figure tilted its head slightly, a small, natural motion that carried no urgency.

"You completed it," it said.

The voice was quiet and clear. Not heard through the air, but understood with the same ease as the earlier message, only now it carried tone, intention, and something unmistakably personal.

Alex felt the difference immediately.

This was not the system.

This was someone.

Bill took a single step forward, measured and unforced. "Yes," he said.

The figure regarded him for a moment longer, as if confirming something already known.

"Most do not," it replied.

Mercer glanced at Alex briefly, then back to the figure. "What is this place?"

The figure did not answer immediately. Its gaze moved across all three of them, not quickly, not analytically, but with a kind of quiet consideration.

"A meeting place," it said at last.

Alex felt that settle more deeply than the words themselves suggested. "You made this?" she asked.

"No," the figure replied gently. "I use it."

Bill's eyes shifted slightly, taking in the structure behind it, the stillness of the patterns, the absence of any further response.

"The system," he said, "it wasn't a defense."

The figure's expression did not change, but something in its posture suggested a soft acknowledgment.

"It was a path," it said.

A brief silence followed.

Alex took a slow breath. "A path to you."

"Yes."

There was no pride in the answer. No emphasis. Only truth.

Mercer's stance eased by a fraction. "And if we hadn't solved it?"

The figure looked at him, not with dismissal, but with clarity.

"Then you would not be here."

Again, no threat. No warning.

Only fact.

Bill studied the figure carefully. "Why create something like this?" he asked.

The figure's gaze returned to him, and for the first time there was something more in it. Not intensity. Not scrutiny.

Interest.

"So that someone who could follow it… would arrive," it said.

The words were simple.

But the meaning behind them was not.

Alex felt something shift quietly within her. All the movement, all the uncertainty, all the complexity they had navigated had not been random.

It had been intentional.

Not to stop them.

To find them.

The space remained still around them, the structure silent, its purpose complete.

And for the first time since stepping through the gate, Alex understood that they had not reached the end of something.

They had been received.

Chapter 28 — What Was Found

The space remained still after the figure spoke.

Alex became aware of how completely the structure had gone quiet. The patterns no longer shifted. The system that had once responded to every movement, every decision, now held no further demand. It had completed its purpose.

The figure stood calmly before them, its presence steady and unforced.

Bill studied it for a moment, then spoke. "You built the path."

The figure tilted its head slightly. "I arranged it."

"For us," Alex said.

"For someone," the figure replied gently. "You are the first in a very long time."

The words did not carry loneliness, but they did carry time.

Mercer shifted his weight, not out of tension now, but out of adjustment. "You've been waiting here?"

"Yes."

Bill glanced briefly at the silent structure behind the figure. "For how long?"

The figure's expression did not change. "Long enough that the difference matters less than the result."

Alex felt that answer settle more deeply than a number ever could.

The figure's gaze moved between them again, slower now, more deliberate. Not studying them as a problem, but regarding them as people.

"You did not force the pattern," it said. "You allowed it to resolve."

Bill gave a small, almost reflexive nod. "It wasn't stable when we tried to control it."

"Yes," the figure replied. "Most try to control it."

A quiet pause followed.

Then the figure stepped forward.

The movement was small, measured, and without any sense of approach or intrusion. It simply reduced the distance between them.

Alex felt no alarm. Only awareness.

The figure stopped first in front of Bill.

For a moment, it said nothing.

It simply looked at him.

Not at his stance. Not at his equipment.

At him.

"You carry the pattern after it is solved," the figure said quietly.

Bill did not respond immediately. His posture remained steady, but something in his expression shifted, as though the words had reached a place he had not expected to be addressed.

"You continue to calculate," the figure continued, "even when there is nothing left to resolve."

Bill exhaled once, slowly. "That's how I make sure it stays solved."

The figure regarded him for a moment longer.

"Yes," it said. "And it is why you succeed."

Another small pause.

"But it is not required… here."

Bill held its gaze. For the first time since they had entered the system, there was no problem in front of him to work, no variable to account for.

The figure's voice softened slightly.

"You are not only what you solve."

The words were simple.

They did not press.

They did not linger.

But they remained.

Bill gave a slight nod, not in agreement alone, but in acknowledgment.

The figure stepped back, then turned its attention to Alex.

She felt the shift immediately.

Not pressure. Not expectation.

Attention.

"You watch," the figure said.

Alex blinked once, surprised by how direct the statement felt.

"You observe before you move," it continued. "You notice what others do not say."

Alex let out a quiet breath. "I try to understand what's happening."

"Yes," the figure said. "And what people are becoming while it happens."

That struck deeper.

Alex hadn't put it into words like that before, but she knew it was true.

The figure studied her for a moment, then spoke again.

"You create space for others to choose."

Alex glanced briefly toward Bill and Mercer, then back.

"I don't always know if I'm helping," she said honestly.

"You are," the figure replied.

No hesitation.

No qualification.

Just certainty.

"That is why they move with you," it added.

Alex felt something settle inside her, not new, but confirmed.

The figure inclined its head slightly, then turned to Mercer.

Mercer stood as he always did—balanced, ready, aware.

The figure observed him for a long moment before speaking.

"You remain prepared," it said.

Mercer gave a short, almost reflexive nod. "That's the job."

"Yes."

The figure stepped a fraction closer.

"Even now."

Mercer's eyes narrowed slightly, not in suspicion, but in thought. "You're saying I don't need to be."

"In this place," the figure replied, "you do not."

The words were not dismissive. They did not deny what he was.

They removed the need for it.

Mercer let out a breath he hadn't realized he was holding. His shoulders eased, not completely, but enough to feel the difference.

"That's… new," he said quietly.

The figure's gaze remained steady.

"You protect," it said. "But protection does not require constant strain."

Mercer considered that, then gave a small nod.

"Maybe I've been doing it that way too long."

"Yes," the figure replied.

There was no judgment in the answer.

Only understanding.

The figure stepped back, returning to a position where it could see all three of them at once.

The space remained quiet.

The structure remained still.

Everything that had been in motion had come to rest.

"You came to understand the pattern," the figure said.

Its voice was calm, almost reflective.

"But I wanted to understand you."

No one spoke.

There was nothing to add to that.

After a moment, Bill looked toward the structure again, then back to the figure. "What happens now?"

The figure considered him, then the space around them.

"You return," it said.

Alex felt a slight shift in the air, not movement, but readiness.

"Will we find this again?" she asked.

The figure's gaze settled on her.

"You know how to listen now," it said. "That is the beginning."

Not a direct answer.

But not an absence of one either.

Mercer glanced around once more. "And this place?"

"It remains," the figure said. "Until it is needed again."

Bill took a slow breath. "And you?"

The figure was quiet for a moment.

"I remain," it said.

Not as a statement of isolation.

As a statement of purpose.

The space around them softened.

Not visibly at first, but perceptibly. The edges of the environment seemed to lose definition, not dissolving, but releasing their hold.

Alex felt it clearly.

The same way she had felt the system before.

But this was different.

There was no test in it.

No evaluation.

Only transition.

The figure remained where it stood.

It did not step back.

It did not disappear.

It simply watched them.

"You completed the path," it said softly.

A final pause.

"And now… you carry it."

The space shifted.

Not through motion, not through light, but through absence.

And then—

They were back.

The surface of Asterra-9 stretched beneath their boots, solid and familiar in a way that required no confirmation. The sky above had returned to its earlier state, dim and distant, with the faint irregularities that had once marked the planet's instability now gone.

Alex inhaled sharply, then steadied herself. There was no disorientation, no aftershock.

Just presence.

Mercer turned slowly in place, scanning the horizon. "We're back."

Bill was already looking outward, his attention moving across the terrain with quiet precision.

"The system is inactive," he said.

Alex followed his gaze.

The structures that had once shifted and responded now stood still. The faint lines that had carried motion and meaning were quiet, their surfaces uniform and unchanging.

"It's still here," she said.

"Yes," Bill replied. "But it's not asking anything anymore."

Mercer let out a low breath. "I'll take that."

A brief silence settled between them.

The planet felt different.

Not because it had changed entirely, but because something had completed.

Alex glanced at Bill. There was something lighter in his posture, not a loss of focus, but a release of weight.

Mercer stood more easily, his stance still ready, but no longer strained.

She felt it too.

Not a shift in what she knew.

A shift in how she held it.

Bill looked once more toward the distant horizon, then turned back.

"We can proceed with the survey," he said.

Alex nodded.

Mercer gave a short, satisfied exhale. "That's the best news I've heard all day."

They began to move, their steps steady and unforced.

Above them, the sky remained unchanged.

The stars, when they would be visible again, would be exactly where they had always been.

But the distance between understanding them and reaching them no longer felt the same.

Not because the universe had changed.

Because they had.

Epilogue — Survey Resumed

The landing zone was quiet.

Not empty, not abandoned, but settled in a way that had not been possible before. The subtle irregularities that had once defined Asterra-9 were gone. The ground held steady. Instruments remained consistent. The small fluctuations that had forced constant recalibration had disappeared completely.

Across the site, survey teams moved with a rhythm that felt almost unfamiliar.

Normal.

Varn stood near the central operations console, reviewing a stream of data as it updated in real time. He had checked the same readings more than once, not because they were unclear, but because they were consistent in a way that required confirmation.

"Still stable?" one of the technicians asked.

Varn didn't look up immediately. He watched the data cycle through another sequence, then another.

"Yes," he said at last. "No drift. No pattern shift. No reactive signatures."

The technician nodded, then turned back to their station. Around them, others resumed their work, mapping, cataloging, measuring. Tasks that had once required caution now proceeded without hesitation.

Asterra-9 had become what it should have been from the beginning.

A surveyable world.

Varn straightened slightly and looked out across the open terrain. The structures that had once moved and responded now stood silent in the distance. Their surfaces were unchanged, but whatever had driven them was no longer active.

He had read the reports.

He had listened to the recordings.

He had spoken briefly with the team after their return.

Everything aligned.

And yet—

He exhaled slowly.

Everything did not explain.

Behind him, footsteps approached.

Varn didn't turn immediately. He already knew who it was.

"You're reviewing it again," Bill said.

Varn allowed a faint, almost amused expression to form. "I am."

He turned then, meeting Bill's gaze.

"It hasn't changed," Varn added. "I thought it might."

"It won't," Bill replied.

There was no uncertainty in his tone.

Varn studied him for a moment. "You're very sure of that."

"Yes."

A brief silence settled between them.

Varn glanced past Bill, where Alex and Mercer stood near the edge of the landing area, speaking quietly with one of the survey teams. They appeared… at ease. Not relaxed in a careless way, but grounded.

Different.

Varn returned his attention to Bill.

"Your report is precise," he said. "You describe the system, the progression, the resolution. You document exactly what changed."

Bill nodded once. "That was the objective."

"Yes," Varn said. "It was."

He paused, then added, "But it doesn't feel complete."

Bill did not respond immediately.

Varn watched him carefully.

"Whatever you encountered beyond the final alignment," Varn continued, "it wasn't just a system, was it?"

The question hung between them, not confrontational, not demanding.

Bill considered it.

He could have answered directly. He could have explained, described, attempted to translate something that had not been given in technical terms.

Instead, he said, "It completed its purpose."

Varn held his gaze a moment longer.

"That's not quite an answer," he said.

"No," Bill agreed. "It isn't."

Another brief silence.

Then Varn nodded once, slowly.

"I didn't think it would be."

There was no frustration in the response. No pressure to push further.

Only acceptance.

Varn glanced once more at the data display, then back across the landscape.

"Whatever it was," he said, "it left the planet in a state we can work with. That's not a small outcome."

"No," Bill said. "It isn't."

Varn folded his arms lightly, considering the horizon.

"We'll continue the survey," he said. "Full mapping. Structural analysis. Environmental baseline. Everything we originally planned."

Bill nodded. "That makes sense."

Varn gave a short, almost thoughtful breath. "And this time, we'll actually be able to finish it."

A faint hint of dry humor touched the words.

Bill allowed the smallest trace of a smile.

"That helps."

Varn looked at him once more, as if weighing whether to say something else.

Then he chose not to.

"Get some rest," he said instead. "You've earned it."

Bill inclined his head slightly. "Understood."

Varn turned back to the console, already moving on to the next sequence of tasks, the work resuming as though it had always been this way.

Bill stepped away, crossing the landing area toward Alex and Mercer.

Mercer noticed him first. "We good?" he asked.

"We're good," Bill replied.

"That's still my favorite outcome," Mercer said.

Alex smiled slightly. "The best one we could have hoped for."

Bill looked past them, toward the distant structures.

They stood exactly where they had been before.

Unchanged.

Inactive.

Silent.

"They're still there," Alex said, following his gaze.

"Yes," Bill replied.

"But whatever was driving them…" she began.

"It's not active," Bill finished.

Mercer crossed his arms loosely. "I'm not going to question that."

Alex glanced at Bill. "Do you think it will come back?"

Bill considered the question.

Then he shook his head slightly. "Not in the same way."

That was all he said.

And it was enough.

A transport signal sounded in the distance as another survey unit moved into position. Equipment was unloaded. Teams coordinated. Voices carried across the open space with a clarity that had not been possible before.

Work had resumed.

Alex took a slow breath, letting it settle.

"It feels different," she said.

Mercer nodded. "Yeah. It does."

Bill looked upward.

The sky above Asterra-9 remained as it had always appeared—dim, distant, without clear reference points. Soon, when they returned to orbit, the stars would come back into view, fixed and familiar.

Unchanged.

And yet—

He knew that was not entirely true.

Not because the stars had moved.

But because distance no longer meant the same thing it had before.

He turned back to the others.

"We should get back," he said.

Alex nodded.

Mercer gave a final glance across the horizon, then followed.

They moved together toward the transport, their pace steady, unforced.

Behind them, the structures remained still.

The system had completed its purpose.

The survey would continue.

The planet would be studied.

The data would be recorded.

But what they had encountered—

what they had been given—

would not be contained in any report.

And though the stars would appear exactly as they always had,

the way they were seen

would not.

Appendix — Mission Addendum: Asterra-9 Survey Log

Classification: Internal Survey Record
Mission Segment: Asterra-9 Surface Expedition
Status: Post-Anomaly Resolution

---

1. Operational Summary

Following the final alignment event at the central structure, all previously observed dynamic behaviors across the Asterra-9 surface ceased.
No further pattern shifts, spatial instability, or reactive structural responses have been recorded.
Surface conditions stabilized immediately and have remained consistent across all subsequent observation cycles.
Survey operations have resumed under standard protocols.

---

2. Structural Observations

The distributed network of surface structures remains physically intact.
All structures previously identified as responsive nodes are now inactive.

- No pattern evolution detected
- No alignment sequences initiated
- No reactive behavior observed in response to proximity, motion, or signal input

The structures retain their geometric configurations and material properties, but no longer exhibit any functional response.
No central control mechanism or processing core has been identified.
All attempts to locate a governing system have yielded negative results.

---

3. Energy and Signal Analysis

Pre-resolution readings indicated non-localized energy distribution across the structural network.

Post-resolution scans show:

- No measurable energy output beyond environmental baseline
- No detectable signal transmission between structures
- No residual field effects consistent with previous system behavior

The transition from active to inactive state occurred without detectable energy discharge, decay pattern, or transitional signature.

Cause of system deactivation remains undetermined.

---

4. Replication Attempts

Multiple controlled attempts have been conducted to reinitiate structural response.

Test parameters included:

- Direct proximity engagement
- Coordinated multi-point positioning
- Signal injection across multiple frequencies
- Pattern reconstruction based on recorded alignment sequences

All attempts produced no response.

The system has not reactivated under any tested condition.

---

5. Environmental Stability

Planetary conditions have normalized across all surveyed regions.

- Surface integrity stable
- No spatial drift detected

- Atmospheric readings consistent
- No anomalous interference with instrumentation

Asterra-9 is now classified as a stable survey environment.
Long-term study and mapping operations are approved.

---

6. Interpretive Notes

The observed system behavior cannot be fully explained by known automated or reactive processes.
Key characteristics include:

- Adaptive response to presence rather than position
- Progressive pattern resolution aligned with participant interaction
- Immediate and complete cessation of activity upon final alignment

The absence of residual systems or identifiable control mechanisms suggests the possibility that the system function was not continuous in nature.
It may have been conditional.

---

7. Addendum — Unfiled Observation

The system no longer responds to input.
However, this does not indicate absence of function.
Only completion.
The final phase of the alignment sequence produced an outcome that cannot be measured, recorded, or independently verified through available instrumentation.
No physical evidence remains.
No system trace can be isolated.
No repeatable process has been identified.
As such, the event is not included in the primary operational report.

Further attempts to initiate the sequence have produced no response.

---

8. Closing Status

Survey operations continue.

All mission objectives remain active.

Asterra-9 is now considered viable for extended study.

No further anomalies have been detected.

End of Addendum

About the Author

Russell McFall writes thoughtful science-fiction stories that explore courage, perseverance, and the quiet choices that shape a life. His work focuses on character, discovery, and the kind of wisdom that grows through experience rather than force.

Before becoming a full-time writer, Russell spent many years in software development, where careful thinking and problem-solving were part of everyday life. Alongside that career, he and his wife devoted years to children's ministry and homeschooling their family—experiences that continue to influence the heart and direction of his stories.

Many of his books began as bedtime adventures told to his children. Over time, those stories grew into larger worlds filled with explorers, distant planets, and characters learning that true strength is often found in patience, compassion, and responsibility.

Russell continues to write with the same sense of wonder that first inspired those early stories.

Also by Russell McFall

Ordained Path Books

Clean Science Fiction and Inspirational Writing for Thoughtful Readers

---

Contemporary Fiction and Short Stories

Stories of Community, Memory, and Hope

- **Squirrel Creek Estates — Where the Porch Lights Stay On**
- **The World That Chose**

The Space Cadet Richard Series

Where the Legacy Began

- **The Final Countdown**
- **The Dunes of Dinkytown**
- **The Mastermind's Maze**

The Space Cadet Legacy Series

Over 30+ novels of courage, friendship, and discovery — including

- **The First Gate**
- **Welcome Back, Player**
- **Flibber's Journey Home**
- **Stronger Together**
- **Phasegate Rising**
- **The Makers' Handshake**
- **Optimized**

(New missions continuing.)

Literary Humor and Reflections

Serious Nonsense — Sanity Sold Separately

Devotional and Reflection Books

- **Remembering God's Help — Stone by Stone**
- **Attributes of God**
- **This Is My Story, This Is My Song**
- **Lives of Faith**
- **Foundations of Faith**

Russell McFall writes clean fiction and thoughtful reflections designed to uplift the heart, sharpen the mind, and remind every reader that light still wins.

www.ingramcontent.com/pod-product-compliance
Lightning Source LLC
LaVergne TN
LVHW010654110826
815149LV00014B/3078